Shirley, Goodness and Mercy

Center Point
Large Print

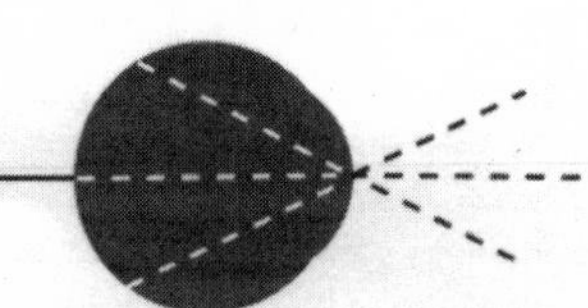

Shirley, Goodness and Mercy

DEBBIE MACOMBER

CENTER POINT PUBLISHING
THORNDIKE, MAINE

This Center Point Large Print edition
is published in the year 2007 by arrangement with
Harlequin Enterprises, Ltd.

The text of this Large Print edition is unabridged. In other
aspects, this book may vary from the original edition.
Printed in the United States of America.
Set in 16-point Times New Roman type.

ISBN-10: 1-60285-052-6
ISBN-13: 978-1-60285-052-1

Library of Congress Cataloging-in-Publication Data

Macomber, Debbie.
Shirley, Goodness and Mercy / Debbie Macomber.--Center Point large print ed.
p. cm.
ISBN-13: 978-1-60285-052-1 (lib. bdg. : alk. paper)
1. Large type books. 2. San Francisco (Calif.)--Fiction. I. Title.

PS3563.A2364S45 2007
813'.54--dc22

2007016315

To my St. Simons Island, Georgia, friends

Becky and Hank Wyrick
Hilaire Bauer
Jackie Randall
and
Phillip DePoy

One

Greg Bennett had always hated Christmas.

He'd never believed in "goodwill toward men" and all that other sentimental garbage. Christmas in the city—any city—was the epitome of commercialism, and San Francisco was no exception. Here it was, barely December, and department-store windows had been filled with automated elves and tinsel-hung Christmas trees since before Thanksgiving!

Most annoying, in Greg's opinion, was the hustle and bustle of holiday shoppers, all of whom seemed to be unnaturally cheerful. That only made his own mood worse.

He wouldn't be in the city at all if he wasn't desperately in need of a bank loan. Without it, he'd be forced to lay off what remained of his crew by the end of the year. He'd have to close the winery's doors. His vines—and literally decades of work—had been wiped out by fan leaf disease, devastating the future of his vineyard and crippling him financially.

He'd spent the morning visiting one financial institution after another. Like a number of other growers, he'd applied at the small-town banks in the Napa Valley and been unsuccessful. His wasn't the only vineyard destroyed by the disease—although, for reasons no one really understood, certain vineyards had been spared the blight. For a while there'd been talk of low-interest loans from the federal government, but they hadn't materialized. Apparently the ruin hadn't been thorough enough to warrant financial assistance. For Greg that news definitely fell into the category of cold comfort.

It left him in a dilemma. No loan—no replanted vines. Without the vines there would be no grapes, without the grapes, no wine, and without the winery, no Gregory Bennett.

What he needed after a morning such as this, he decided, was a good stiff drink and the company of a charming female companion, someone who could help him forget his current troubles. He walked into the St. Francis, the elegant San Francisco hotel, and found himself facing a twenty-foot Christmas tree decorated with huge gold balls and plush red velvet bows. Disgusted, he looked away and hurried toward the bar.

The bartender seemed to sense his urgency. "What can I get you?" he asked promptly. He wore a name tag that identified him as Don.

Greg sat down on a stool. "Get me a martini," he said. If it hadn't been so early in the day, he would have asked for a double, but it was barely noon and he still had to drive home. He didn't feel any compelling reason to return. The house, along with everything else in his life, was empty. Oh, the furniture was all there—Tess hadn't taken that—but he was alone, more alone than he could ever remember being.

Tess, his third and greediest wife, had left him six months earlier. The attorneys were fighting out the details of their divorce, and at three hundred dollars an hour, neither lawyer had much incentive to rush into court.

Nevertheless, Tess was gone. He silently toasted eliminating her from his life and vowed not to make the mistake of marrying again. Three wives was surely sufficient evidence that he wasn't the stay-married kind.

Yet he missed Tess, he mused with some regret—and surprise. Well, maybe not Tess exactly, but a warm body in his bed. By his side. Even at the time, he'd known it was foolish to marry her. He certainly *should* have known, after the messy end of his second marriage. His first had lasted ten years, and he'd split with Jacquie over . . . Hell if he could remember. Something stupid. It'd always been something stupid.

"You out shopping?" Don the bartender asked as he delivered a bowl of peanuts.

Greg snorted. "Not on your life."

The younger man smiled knowingly. "Ah, you're one of those."

"You mean someone who's got common sense. What is it with people and Christmas? Normal, sane human beings become sentimental idiots." A year ago, when he and Tess had been married less than eighteen months, she'd made it clear she expected diamonds for Christmas. Lots of them. She'd wanted him to make her the envy of her friends. That was what he got for marrying a woman nineteen years his junior. A pretty blonde with a figure that could stop traffic. Next time around he'd simply move the woman into his house and send her packing when he grew bored with her. No more marriages—not for him. He didn't need any more legal entanglements.

Just then a blond beauty entered the bar, and Greg did a double take. For half a heartbeat, he thought it was Tess. Thankfully he was wrong. Blond, beautiful and probably a bitch. The last part didn't bother him, though—especially now, when he could use a little distraction. He'd be sixty-one his next birthday, but he was trim and fit, and still had all his hair—gone mostly gray, what people called "distinguished." In fact, he could easily pass for ten years younger. His good looks had taken him a long way in this world, and he'd worked hard to maintain a youthful appearance.

"Welcome," he greeted her, swerving around on his stool to give her his full attention.

"Hello."

Her answering smile told him she wasn't averse to his company. Yes, she might well provide a distraction. If everything worked out, he might stay in town overnight. Considering the morning he'd had, he deserved a little comfort. He wasn't interested in anything serious—just a light flirtation to take his mind off his troubles, a dalliance to momentarily distract him.

"Are you meeting someone?" Greg asked.

"Not really," she said, her voice sultry and deep.

Greg noted the packages. "Been shopping, I see."

She nodded, and when the bartender walked over to her table, Greg said, "Put it on my tab."

"Thanks," she said in that same sultry voice. He was even more impressed when she asked for a glass of Bennett Wine. A pinot noir.

He slipped off the stool and approached her table. "I'm Greg."

"Cherry Adams."

He liked her name; it suited her. "Do you mind if I join you?"

"Go ahead. Why not?"

The day was already looking brighter. He pulled out a chair and sat down. They made small talk for a few minutes, exchanged pleasantries. He didn't mention his last name because he didn't want her to make the connection and have their conversation weighed down by the problems at Bennett Wines. However, it soon became clear that she was knowledgeable about wine—and very flattering about his 1996 pinot noir. Tess had been an idiot on the subject, despite being married to the owner of a winery. She didn't know the difference between chablis and chardonnay. And she never did understand why he couldn't call his own sparkling wine champagne, no matter how many times he told her the name could only be used for sparkling wines from the Champagne region of France.

After another glass of wine for her and a second martini for him, Greg suggested lunch. Cherry hesitated and gazed down at her hands. "Sorry, but I've got a nail appointment."

"You could cancel it," Greg suggested, trying to hint

that they could find more entertaining ways to occupy themselves. He didn't want her to think he was being pushy. Later, after lunch, he'd surprise her and announce who he really was. He was pleased—no, delighted—by her interest in him, particularly because she didn't know he was the man responsible for the wine she'd described as "exquisite." He grinned; wait till he told her. Cherry's interest proved what he'd been telling himself ever since Tess had walked out on him. He was still young, still vital, still sexy.

That was when it happened.

The look that crossed Cherry's face conveyed her thoughts as clearly as if she'd said them aloud. She wasn't interested. Oh, sure, he was good for a few drinks, especially since he was buying. Good for an hour of conversation. But that was all.

"I really do have to go," Cherry said as she reached for her shopping bags. "My nails are a mess. Thanks for the, uh, company and the wine, though."

"Don't mention it," Greg muttered, watching her leave. He was still reeling from the blow to his pride.

Soon afterward, he left, too. He'd never been one to take rejection well, mainly because he'd had so little experience of it.

After two martinis he knew he wasn't in any condition to drive. So he left his car in the lot and started to walk. With no destination in mind, he wandered down the crowded street, trying to keep his distance from all those happy little shoppers. His stomach growled and his head hurt, but not nearly as much as his ego. Every time he thought about the look on Cherry's face, he cringed. Okay, okay, she'd been too young. At a guess he'd say she was no more than thirty.

However, Greg knew a dozen women her age who would leap at the opportunity to spend a day and a night with him. He was suave, sophisticated and rich. Not as rich as he'd once been—would be again, as soon as he got this latest mess straightened out. *If* he got it straightened out. The truth was, he stood on the brink of losing everything.

Desperate to escape his dark thoughts, he began to walk at a brisker pace. He made an effort not to think, not to acknowledge his fears and worries, concentrating, instead, on the movement of his feet, the rhythm of his breath. He turned corner after corner and eventually found himself on a side street dominated by an imposing brick church.

He paused in front of it. A church. Now that was a laugh. He remembered how his mother had dragged him and his brother, Phil, to service every Sunday. He'd even attended services while he was in college. But he hadn't darkened the door of a church since . . . Catherine.

She'd been his sweetheart, his *lover,* during college—until he'd broken it off. No, abandoned her. That was a more honest description of what he'd done. The years had numbed his guilt, and he rarely thought of her anymore. Funny how a relationship that had ended more than thirty-five years ago could suddenly rise up to haunt him. He'd been a senior the last time he'd seen

Catherine. They'd been madly in love. Then she'd told him she was pregnant and Greg had panicked. About to graduate, about to start his life, he'd done what had seemed sensible at the time; he'd fled.

Unable to face her, he'd written Catherine a letter and told her he was leaving. She should do whatever she wanted about the baby. It'd been cowardly of him, but he was just a kid back then; he'd long since stopped berating himself over it. He'd never heard from her again. He didn't know what she'd done about the baby. Didn't want to know. Abortions hadn't been legal at the time, but there were ways of getting rid of an unwanted pregnancy even then. His mother hadn't ever learned why his relationship with Catherine had ended, but Phil knew. That was the beginning of the estrangement between Greg and his brother.

Almost without realizing it, Greg began to move up the church steps. He blamed it on the throng of shoppers crowding in around him. All he wanted was a few moments of peace and quiet. A chance to think.

He hesitated on the top step. He didn't belong in a church, not the way he'd lived. And yet . . .

His life was empty and he was old enough to recognize that. But at sixty, it was a bit late. For most of his adult life, he'd followed the path of least resistance, put his own interests above those of other people. He'd believed that was the basis of prosperity, of success. Deserting Catherine was where it had started.

She'd been the first of his regrets. Matthias was the second. And then his mother . . .

Matthias Jamison was his father's cousin and an employee at the winery. Greg's parents had divorced when he was in high school, and he and Phil had spent summers with their father at the vineyard. Although the younger of the two, Greg was the one who'd been drawn to the family business. He'd spent hour after hour there, learning everything he could about wine and wine making.

Ten years his senior, Matthias had taken Greg under his wing. What John Bennett didn't teach Greg about wine making, Matthias did. His father had also insisted Greg get a business degree, and he'd been right. Several years later, when he died, Greg bought out Phil's half to become sole owner and worked with Matthias operating the winery.

The wine had always been good. What the business needed was an aggressive advertising campaign. People couldn't order the Bennett label if they'd never heard of it. The difficulty with Greg's ideas was the huge financial investment they demanded. Commissioning sophisticated full-page ads and placing them in upscale food magazines, attending wine expositions throughout the world—it had all cost money. He'd taken a gamble, which was just starting to pay off when Matthias came to him, needing a loan.

Mary, Matthias's wife of many years, had developed a rare form of blood cancer. The experimental drug that might save her life wasn't covered by their health insurance. The cost of the medication was threatening to bankrupt Matthias; his savings were gone and no bank would lend him money. He'd asked Greg for help. After everything the older man had done for him and for his family, Greg knew he owed Matthias that and more.

The decision had been agonizing. Bennett Wines was just beginning to gain recognition; sales had doubled and tripled. But Greg's plans were bigger than that. He'd wanted to help Matthias, but there was no guarantee the treatment would be effective. So he'd turned Matthias down. Mary had died a few months later, when conventional treatments failed, and a bitter Matthias had left Bennett Wines and moved to Washington state.

Generally Greg didn't encourage friendships. He tended to believe that friends took advantage of you, that they resented your success. It was every man for himself, in Greg's view. Still, Matthias had been the best friend he'd ever had. Because of what happened, the two men hadn't spoken in fifteen years.

Greg could have used Matthias's expertise in dealing with the blight that had struck his vines, but he was too proud to give him the opportunity to slam the door in his face. To refuse him the way he'd refused Matthias all those years ago.

No, Greg definitely wasn't church material. Whatever had possessed him to think he should go into this place, seek solace here, he couldn't fathom.

He was about to turn away when he noticed that the church doors were wide open. Had they been open all this time? He supposed they must have been. It was almost as if he was being invited inside. . . . He shook his head, wondering where *that* ridiculous thought had come from. Nevertheless, he slowly walked in.

The interior was dim and his eyes took a moment to adjust. He saw that the sanctuary was huge, with two rows of pews facing a wide altar. Even the church was decorated for the holidays. Pots of red and white poinsettias were arranged on the altar, and a row of gaily decorated Christmas trees stood behind it. A large cross hung suspended from the ceiling.

An organ sat off to one side, along with a sectioned space for the choir. Greg hadn't stopped to notice which denomination this church was. Nor did he care.

Although his mother had been an ardent churchgoer, Greg had hated it, found it meaningless. But Phil seemed to eat this religious stuff up, just like their mother had.

"Okay," Greg said aloud. None of this whispering business for him. "The door was open. I came inside. You want me to tell you I made a mess of my life? Fine, I screwed up. I could've done better. Is that what you were waiting to hear? Is that what you wanted me to say? I said it. Are you happy now?"

His words reverberated, causing him to retreat a step.

And as he did, his life suddenly overwhelmed him. His failures, his shortcomings, his mistakes came roaring at him like an avalanche, jerking him off his feet. He seemed to tumble backward through the years. The force of it was too much and he slumped into a pew, the weight of his past impossible to bear. He leaned forward and buried his face in his hands.

"Can you forgive me, Mama?" he whispered brokenly. "Is there any way I can make up for what I did—not being there for you? When you needed me . . ."

He deserved every rotten thing that was happening to him. If he couldn't get a loan, if he lost the winery, it would be what he deserved. All of it.

Greg wouldn't have recognized his words as a prayer. But, they wove their way upward, past the church altar, past the suspended crucifix, toward the bell tower and church steeple. Once free of the building, they flew heavenward, through the clouds and beyond the sky, landing with a crash on the cluttered desk of the Archangel Gabriel.

"Well, well," the archangel said, a little surprised and more than a little pleased. "What do we have here?"

Two

The Archangel Gabriel arched his white brows as he reviewed Greg Bennett's file. A very thick file. "Well, it's about time," he muttered, and dutifully recorded the prayer request.

"I certainly agree with you there," a soft female voice murmured in response.

Gabriel didn't have to look up to see who'd joined him. That angelic voice was all too familiar. Shirley was visiting, and where Shirley was, Goodness and Mercy were sure to follow. His three favorite trouble-makers—heaven help him. Without having to ask, he knew what she wanted. The trio had been pestering him for three years about a return trip to earth.

"Hello, Shirley," Gabriel said without much enthusiasm. The truth was, he'd always been partial to Shirley, Goodness and Mercy, although he dared not let it show. Their escapades on earth were notorious in the corridors of paradise and had created an uproar on more than one occasion.

"We've decided you seem frazzled," Goodness said, popping up next to her friend. She rested her arms on Gabriel's desk, studying him avidly.

"Overworked," Mercy agreed, appearing beside the other two.

"And we're here to help." Shirley walked around the front of his desk and gave him a pitying look.

"We feel your pain," Goodness told him.

If she hadn't sounded so sincere, Gabriel would have laughed outright. He was still tempted to tell her to cut the psychobabble, but knew that wouldn't do any good. As it was, he sighed and leaned back in his chair.

"So—what *can* we do to help?" Mercy inquired with a serenity few would question.

"Help?" he asked. "You can help me most by participating in the heavenly host again this year."

"We've already done that for three years," Goodness complained with a slight pout, crossing her arms. "It's just no fun to be one in a cast of thousands."

"We want to go back to earth," Shirley explained. Of the three, she was the most plainspoken. Gabriel knew he could count on her to tell him the truth. She did her utmost to keep the other two in line, but could only hold out for so long before she succumbed to temptation herself.

"I love humans," Goodness said, hands clasped as she gazed longingly toward earth.

"Me, too," Mercy was quick to add. "Where else in the universe would anyone assume God is dead and Elvis is alive?"

Gabriel successfully hid a smile. "Even with the best of intentions, you three have never been able to keep your wings to yourselves."

"True." Shirley nodded in agreement. "But remember we're angels, not saints."

"All the more reason to make you stay in heaven where you belong," Gabriel argued.

The objections came fast and furious.

"But you need us this year!"

"More than ever, Gabriel. You've got far more work than you can handle!"

"You're overburdened!"

True enough. As always, Christmas was his busiest time of year, and Gabriel's desk was flooded with thousands upon thousands of prayer requests. No denying it, human beings were the most difficult of God's subjects. Obtuse, demanding and contrary. Many of them flung prayer requests at heaven without once considering that humans played a role in solving their own problems. The hard part was getting them to recognize that they had lessons to learn before their prayer requests could be granted. God-directed solutions often came from within themselves. Gabriel's task, with the help of his other prayer ambassadors, was to show these proud stubborn creatures the way.

"Do you have any requests from children?" Shirley asked. As a former guardian angel, she enjoyed working with youngsters the most.

"Anyone in need of a little Mercy?" Mercy prodded.

"Any good faithful souls who could use a bit of angelic guidance?" Goodness asked.

"Here," Gabriel said abruptly as he shoved Greg Bennett's prayer request at them.

Gabriel didn't know what had possessed him. Frustration, perhaps. Then again, it could have been something far more powerful. It could have been the very hand of God. "This request will require all three of you. Read it over, do your homework and get back to me. You might decide that singing with the heavenly host doesn't sound so bad, after all."

He grinned sheepishly as they fluttered away, eager to discover everything they could about this sad human and the sorry mess he'd made of his life.

In truth Gabriel half expected they'd choose to return to the heavenly choir; if they did he wouldn't blame them. Greg Bennett's case would be a challenge for the most experienced prayer ambassadors—let alone these three. Once Shirley, Goodness and Mercy had the opportunity to read his file, they were bound to see that.

• • •

The trio gathered around the file detailing the life of Greg Bennett. Shirley noted that their excited chatter had quickly died down as they read. The oldest and most mature, she could see through Gabriel's ploy. The archangel expected them to give up before they started. To tell him how right he was and scurry back to choir practice. In light of what she'd learned about Greg Bennett, perhaps that would be for the best.

"Oh, my," Goodness whispered. "He abandoned his college sweetheart when she was pregnant."

"Deserted his best friend in his hour of need."

"Look what he did to his own *mother!*"

"To his mother?"

Shirley nodded. "Greg Bennett is a—"

"Scumbag," Mercy supplied.

"He's arrogant."

"Selfish."

"And conceited."

"It's going to take a whole bunch of miracles to whip this poor boy into shape."

Shirley had no argument there. "I'm afraid Greg Bennett is more than any of us could handle," she said sadly.

Goodness and Mercy glanced at each other. "She's joking, isn't she?"

"No, I'm not," Shirley said on a disparaging note. "You read for yourself what kind of man he is. Frankly, I feel someone else, someone who's got more experience with humans and their frailties, would be better equipped to deal with the likes of Mr. Bennett."

"Oh, fiddlesticks!" Goodness cried.

"We can do it," Mercy contended with considerably more confidence than the success of her earlier exploits might have warranted.

"We all know Gabriel did this on purpose," Goodness said. Apparently she hadn't been fooled, either. "He assumed that once we see what a mess Greg's made of his life, we'll figure it's hopeless and slink back to the choir. Well, I, for one, have no intention of spending another Christmas singing my lungs out over the fields of Bethlehem. To be so close to earth and yet so far . . ."

Mercy giggled but appeared to be in full agreement. "Come on, Shirley, this is our one and only chance to return to earth. Okay, so you're right. Greg Bennett isn't exactly a believer in God's love, but God does love him. Heaven knows he needs help."

Shirley was adamant. "More than we can give him."

"Don't be such a pessimist," Goodness chided. "If nothing else, we can steer him in the right direction."

"San Francisco," Mercy said, tapping her cheek. "There are ships in San Francisco, aren't there?"

Shirley could already see trouble brewing. "You've got to promise to stay away from the shipyard," she said heatedly. It'd taken them years to live down what had happened at the Bremerton Naval Shipyard in Washington state. The news crew that covered the repositioning of two aircraft carriers might as well have been reporting directly to heaven, what with all the attention the incident had received.

"Okay, I promise, no shipyard," Mercy said. Shirley was appeased until she thought she saw her fellow angel wink at Goodness. Oh, my, if they took the Bennett case, then this was going to be some Christmas. On the other hand . . .

"Where are you headed?" Goodness called out when Shirley broke away.

"I'm going back to tell Gabriel we'll take the job. Just don't make me sorry I agreed to this."

"Would we do that?" Mercy asked, the picture of angelic innocence.

Shirley had a very good reason for feeling skeptical, but an even better reason for tackling this stint on earth. She wanted out of the choir as much as her two friends did. A human, even one who happened to have more than his share of frailties, wasn't going to stop her.

"Hi, Dad!" Michael Thorpe bounded enthusiastically into the hospital clinic, his eyes sparkling.

Dr. Edward Thorpe looked up from the chart he was reading and smiled at the sight of his son. His wife, Janice, five months pregnant, hurried to keep up with the energetic boy.

The six-year-old raced into his arms and Edward lifted him high above his head. Seeing his own healthy happy son was exactly what he needed. Much of his morning had been spent with another youngster, Tanner Westley, who was ten and suffering from a rare form of leukemia. Edward was an oncologist who specialized in childhood cancers; his work had recently garnered the interest of the *San Francisco Herald.* Just today, a reporter had interviewed him for a piece the paper was running on the urgent need for bone marrow donors. The story would include a photograph of Tanner. Most members of the public didn't seem to understand that they had the opportunity to save lives by testing to become donors. The only thing required at this stage was a simple blood test. The article would make a strongly worded plea for bone marrow donors to help children such as Tanner.

The reporter felt the timing was good. People seemed more generous with their time and money over the Christmas period. Edward hoped they'd be equally giving about submitting to a blood test.

"Hello, darling," his wife said.

"Is it lunchtime already?" With the interview and Tanner Westley's additional tests, his morning had flown.

Janice glanced at her watch. "Actually, we're late."

"Mom and I were shopping." Michael rolled his eyes as if to say how much that had bored him. Edward hid a smile. An intolerance for shopping was something he had in common with his son.

"Can you still join us for lunch?" Janice asked.

Now it was Edward's turn to glance at his watch. "If you don't mind eating in the cafeteria." He needed to be within a few minutes of Tanner, who was starting a new chemotherapy session today.

"We can eat in the cafeteria, can't we, Mom?" Michael tugged at his mother's arm. "Their ice-cream machine is way cool."

"Okay—I'm convinced," Janice responded good-naturedly as the three of them headed toward the elevator.

"Why are we here?" Goodness demanded, her voice unnaturally high. "You *know* I don't like hospitals."

"I didn't bring us here. Shirley did."

"Would you two stop it?" Shirley sighed in exasperation. Goodness and Mercy were enough to try the patience of a saint, let alone another angel. "That's Greg Bennett's son."

"Which one?"

"The cancer specialist," Shirley said, thinking it should have been obvious.

"You mean he's Catherine's child?"

"Right." It was Gabriel who'd directed her to the hospital, but she hadn't told the others that. As far as she was concerned, they would receive information strictly on a need-to-know basis. It was safer that way.

"But he's wonderful!"

"Unlike his birth father," Goodness said under her breath.

Shirley agreed completely. "Greg Bennett broke Catherine's heart, you know." The file had told her that, and ever since, she'd found it a struggle to care in the slightest about Greg and his vineyard.

"She loved him deeply," Mercy added, shaking her

head. "When Greg turned his back on her, she was devastated."

"Then she gave birth to Edward and raised him on her own, and had trouble trusting men again for a very long time."

"She didn't marry until Edward was nearly eight." Shirley recounted the facts as she remembered them. "But she's very happy now. . . ."

"Does she have other children?"

"A daughter, who's a child psychologist," Shirley supplied. "They meet every Friday for lunch on Fisherman's Wharf."

"That's on the waterfront, isn't it?" Mercy brightened.

Shirley cast her fellow angel a quelling look. She didn't want to say it, but Mercy's obsession with ships was beginning to bother her. Oh, my, she didn't know how she was going to get through this holiday season with Goodness and Mercy and still have any kind of effect on Greg Bennett. As much fun as it was to enjoy the things of this earth, they were on an important mission and didn't have time to get sidetracked.

"Meanwhile, Greg has had three wives and each one of them looks exactly like Catherine," Goodness pointed out.

Shirley hadn't recognized that, but as soon as Goodness made the observation, she knew it was true. "Only he doesn't see there's a pattern here," she murmured.

"He hasn't opened his eyes wide enough to see it," Goodness said.

"Yet." Mercy crossed her arms in a determined way that seemed to suggest she'd take great delight in telling him.

"Yet?" Shirley raised her eyebrows in warning, but continued her summary of Greg's failings. "His only child, a son he deserted before he was born, grew up to become a noted cancer specialist, while Greg has squandered his life on wine and women."

"Yes, and while he was trying to pick up some blond babe in a fancy bar, Edward was treating a ten-year-old leukemia patient," Mercy said in a scornful voice.

Goodness grew quiet, which was always a dangerous sign.

"What are you thinking?" Shirley asked her.

"I'm thinking about Catherine," Goodness confessed.

"He hasn't seen her since college," Shirley put in.

"But it seems to me that Greg's been searching for her in every woman he's met," Goodness said thoughtfully.

"Certainly every woman he marries," Mercy added, not concealing her disgust.

"And?" Shirley prodded. "What's your point, Goodness?"

"Well . . . perhaps we should do something to help make it happen."

"What do you mean?"

"Well, if he's looking for Catherine, which he *seems* to be doing, we can make sure he finds her. He should see what she's done with her life, how happy she is . . ."

"Goodness, I don't think that's such a good idea,"

Shirley protested. "You know the rules as well as I do, and we're not supposed to interfere in human lives."

"Who said anything about interfering?"

"There isn't any rule against sending humans in a particular direction, is there?" Mercy asked.

"No, but . . ." Shirley began. Goodness and Mercy, however, had disappeared before the words left her lips.

Oh, dear. Already it was starting. Already she'd lost control.

Shirley raced after the other two, hoping she could stop them in time.

Three

Greg had remained in the church longer than he'd intended. He felt a little foolish sitting there in that quiet darkened place all alone. It was almost as if . . . as if he was waiting for something to happen. Or for someone to appear and speak to him—which, of course, was ridiculous. God was hardly going to drop down and have a heart-to-heart with someone like him.

Other than that unaccountable feeling of anticipation, nothing out of the ordinary had occurred during the time he'd been in this church. Nevertheless, the experience had calmed him. For that half hour, Greg was able to set his troubles aside. He'd never been one to dwell on the negatives; it was far easier to push his regrets and worries from his mind, pretend they didn't exist. Anyway, he'd always managed to surmount his business problems, even when the vineyard had suffered from other disasters—flooding or frost or even fire.

Only this time he had a gut feeling that there wasn't going to be any last-minute rescue. This one was different. If some kind of solution didn't turn up soon, he was going to lose everything.

At sixty he was too old to start over.

After he left the church, he began walking again, his thoughts heavy. It probably wasn't a good idea to drive yet, so he aimlessly wandered the streets. He considered the few options he had. He could declare bankruptcy. Or he could throw himself on his brother's mercy. Phil had become a vice president of Pacific Union, one of the largest banks in the state. He could certainly pull strings to help Greg secure a loan.

But they hadn't spoken since their mother's death. Greg didn't blame Phil for hating him, especially after what he'd done. Another regret. Another person who'd needed him—another person he'd failed. His own mother.

A sick feeling settled over him. He increased his pace as if he could outdistance his guilt. His mother might have forgiven him, but his brother hadn't. Their quarrel following the funeral had ended any chance Greg might have had of receiving Phil's help now.

Although he wasn't hungry, Greg decided to find some lunch. With food in his stomach to cut the effects of the alcohol, he could safely drive, and empty though it was, home had begun to seem mighty appealing.

He could buy a cup of chowder or a seafood sandwich along Fisherman's Wharf, so he hurried downhill toward the waterfront, his pace filled with sudden purpose. The wind was cold and brisk, and he gathered his coat around him as he neared the wharf. What on earth were all these people doing here? No doubt spending their money on useless junk for Christmas. Grumbling, he wove his way through the crowds toward the closest fish bar.

"There she is," Goodness whispered, pressing her face against the restaurant window.

"You found her?" Mercy sounded incredulous as she peered in the window, too. "Oh, my, Catherine really is lovely."

Shirley couldn't resist. She cupped her hands about her face and gazed through the smudged glass, too.

"Her daughter looks exactly like her," Mercy said.

Her friends were right, Shirley thought. Catherine was a classic beauty who carried herself with grace and elegance. Her daughter, whose name was Carrie, if she remembered correctly, strongly resembled her mother. It was like turning back the clock and seeing Catherine as the young college student who had loved and trusted Greg Bennett.

Shirley pinched her lips, disliking Greg Bennett more than ever. She wasn't one to suffer fools gladly.

"Greg Bennett needs a lot of help," she said, disheartened that their angelic talents were being wasted on a man who would neither acknowledge nor appreciate their endeavors.

Shirley figured that if the three of them stood directly in front of him in a full display of God's glory, Greg would turn around and head in the opposite direction.

"I bet Catherine didn't think so at the time, but the fact that Greg Bennett walked out on her was probably the best thing that could've happened. He's been a rotten husband to all three of his wives." Goodness shook her head in disgust. Apparently, she, too, was having difficulty finding him worthy of their assistance.

"What I don't understand," Mercy said, her expression thoughtful, "is why Gabriel would assign us someone who's so . . ." She floundered.

Goodness finished the sentence for her. "Impossible," she said. "Greg Bennett's *impossible.* And he doesn't care about God."

"But as we've discussed before, God cares about him, and so does Gabriel. Greg Bennett is the reason we're here," Shirley said. "The reason we had an opportunity to return to earth. It's our duty to make sure this is a Christmas he'll remember."

Both Goodness and Mercy stepped aside as Catherine and her daughter walked out of the restaurant, laughing and talking animatedly.

"You're right," Goodness agreed once mother and daughter had passed. "I don't like Greg Bennett any more than either of you, but God loves him." She began to say something else, then stopped abruptly. Her deep blue eyes grew huge. "Oh—look at that!"

"At what?" Shirley demanded.

"You'll never guess who's here," Goodness said excitedly. "Right now!"

Shirley whirled about, almost afraid to look. It couldn't be—but she knew it had to be. "Greg Bennett."

"We've got to *do* something," Mercy insisted. "Think, everyone. We can't let an opportunity like this pass."

"No . . . no!" Shirley cried, but Goodness and Mercy were already moving toward a table covered with steaming cooked crabs. "Not the crabs," but it was too late.

These Friday luncheon dates with her daughter were a delightful part of Catherine Thorpe's week. The hour with Carrie always went by in a flash. Meeting her daughter gave her an excuse to linger in the downtown area, as well. San Francisco in December was a sight to behold, and she planned to finish up her afternoon with some holiday shopping. She loved spoiling her grandson, and with another grandchild due in April, her world was full.

"I'll see you and Dad on Sunday, then," Carrie said as they strolled toward her office building.

"Bring Jason with you," Catherine urged. She knew her daughter well enough to recognize that her current boyfriend was someone special.

"Mother," Carrie chided, "I don't—"

She was interrupted by a terrible clang. For no apparent reason, a table full of freshly cooked crabs toppled over, scattering them in every direction. Most of the contents slid across the pavement toward a strikingly attractive older man who leaped out of the way with enviable dexterity.

Catherine recognized Greg instantly, but she soon discovered that his gaze was focused on Carrie. He frowned, as if confused.

"Catherine?"

Carrie turned toward her mother and Greg's gaze followed. Catherine looked him full in the face, was looking at him for the first time in thirty-five years. Her lungs felt frozen and for a moment she couldn't breathe.

So this was Greg.

During the past decades Catherine had sometimes wondered how she'd react if she ever saw him again. Now she knew. Her mouth went dry, and the remembered pain of what he'd done made it difficult to swallow.

"Mom?"

Carne's voice sounded as if it was coming from a great distance.

Catherine had to make a concerted effort to pull her attention back to her daughter.

"You look like you've seen a ghost," Carrie said worriedly.

"I'm fine," Catherine assured her daughter, but in

fact, she *was* seeing a ghost. The ghost of a man who had destroyed her ability to love and trust. Time had dulled her bitterness toward Greg Bennett, had changed her feelings, but even all these years couldn't minimize the shock of seeing him so unexpectedly.

Before she could decide if she should approach Greg or ignore him, he took a step toward her, then hesitated. Catherine remained still. He slowly came closer until they stood face-to-face.

A flurry of activity went on about them as several people scurried to pick up the spilled crabs, but Catherine barely noticed.

"Catherine." Greg's voice was low, a little shaky.

"You know my mother?" Carrie asked, taking Catherine's arm protectively.

"Greg's an old friend," Catherine explained when it became apparent that Greg wasn't answering. She saw the way he stared at her daughter, and then she understood why. "Greg, this is my twenty-five-year-old daughter, Carrie Thorpe."

He picked up her message quickly. This wasn't his child, his daughter, and to his credit his recovery was smooth. "You're just as beautiful as your mother. When I first saw you I thought you *were* your mother."

Carrie blushed at the praise. "People tell me that all the time." She suddenly glanced at her watch. "Oh, no. I hope you'll forgive me, but I have to rush back to work."

"Of course," Greg said as Carrie turned away.

"Goodbye, darling," Catherine called after her. "We'll see you and Jason Sunday for dinner."

When she was gone, Catherine looked at Greg. She'd always known this might happen, that she'd encounter Greg again, but now that she had, she wasn't sure what to do or what to say.

Greg seemed equally flustered. "It's been . . . a lot of years."

She gave a quick nod.

"Would you care to sit down?" he asked, then offered her a shaky smile. "Frankly, my knees feel like they're about to give out on me."

Catherine didn't feel much steadier herself.

"That sounds like a good idea."

Greg led her to a sidewalk café, and when the waiter appeared, he ordered coffee for both of them. Although she normally drank her coffee black, Catherine added sugar to help her recover from the shock.

"Does Carrie have any older siblings?" Greg asked after a moment of stilted silence.

"A brother . . . I . . . had a boy seven months after you left," she said.

"You kept the baby?"

"Yes."

"You raised him?"

"Yes."

"Alone?"

She merely nodded this time, her throat thickening with the memory of the hardships she'd endured in those early years—the long hours, the hard work, the sleepless nights. "I . . . married when Edward was eight," she managed after a while, "and a year later Larry adopted him."

"So I have a son."

"No," Catherine told him, but without malice. "You are the biological father of a child. A wonderful young man who matured without the opportunity of ever knowing you. Without your ever knowing him."

Greg stared down at his coffee. "I was young. Stupid."

"Afraid," Catherine added softly. "We both were."

"But you weren't the one who ran away."

Catherine's laugh was wry. "I couldn't. I was the one carrying the baby."

Greg briefly closed his eyes. "I regret what I did, Catherine. I wanted to know what happened, but was afraid to find out."

"I know."

He looked at her then, as if he found it difficult to believe what she was saying.

Catherine glanced away. "It happened a very long time ago."

"I'm so sorry." He choked out the words, his voice raw with emotion.

"Don't say it," she whispered.

His face revealed his doubt, his confusion.

"You don't need to apologize, Greg. I forgave you years ago. You didn't realize it at the time and neither did I, but you gave me a beautiful gift in Edward. He was a wonderful child and a joy to my parents, who helped me raise him those first few years."

"You moved back home?"

"Until the baby was born. Then Mom watched him for me during the day while I finished college."

"It must have been difficult for you."

"It was." Catherine wasn't going to minimize the sacrifices demanded of her as a single mother. Those years had been bleak.

"Edward," Greg said. "After your father."

Catherine nodded, surprised he'd remembered her father's name.

"How could you forgive me?" Greg asked, sounding almost angry that she didn't harbor some deep resentment toward him. It was as if he expected her to punish him, to mete out her own form of justice right then and there.

"I had to forgive you, Greg, before I could get on with my life. After a while, the bitterness was more than I could endure. I had to leave it behind, and once I did, I discovered a true freedom. Soon afterward, I met Larry. We've been married for twenty-seven years now."

"But I don't deserve your forgiveness."

"That's not for me to say. But don't think forgiving you was easy, because it wasn't. When I first heard you'd left, I refused to accept it. I read your letter over and over—even though I couldn't take it in. I was convinced you'd be back. All you needed was time to sort everything out. I told myself you'd return to me and everything would be all right . . . but I had a rude awakening."

"I . . . wasn't ready to be a father. I guess I never was."

Catherine wondered if she'd misunderstood him. "You mean to say you never had children?"

"None," he said. "Three wives, but not one of them was interested in a family. For that matter, neither was I." He hesitated and his gaze skirted hers. "I was a selfish bastard when I left you. Unfortunately that hasn't changed."

She couldn't confirm or deny his words, for she no longer knew him.

"Would you mind telling me about Edward?" he asked.

Catherine leaned back and sipped her coffee. "In many ways he's very like you. The physical resemblance is there, anyway."

Greg looked up and smiled faintly.

"He's six-two and muscular."

"How old? Thirty-four?"

"Thirty-five," she told him. "His birthday was last month on the twenty-ninth."

"Is he married?"

"Yes, and he has a son himself and another baby on the way. Next spring."

Greg's smile grew wider.

"He's a doctor."

"Really?" Greg seemed to have trouble believing it.

"My husband is, too." Perhaps it was time to remind

Greg who Edward's father was. "Larry raised Edward, helped make him the kind of man he is. Larry's his father."

Greg shook his head. "I wouldn't interfere in his life."

It took a moment for his words to sink in—and then it occurred to her what he'd meant. "Are you asking to meet Edward?"

Greg didn't respond for a long time. His face pale and intent, he finally said, "Yes. Could I?"

Four

Matthias Jamison enjoyed puttering around in his greenhouse before breakfast. The mornings—that was when he missed Mary the most. She'd been gone fifteen years now, and not a day passed that he didn't think about the woman he'd loved for more than thirty years. Some men he'd known were quick to remarry after losing their wives. Not him. Mary had been the only woman for him, and no one else would ever fill the void left by her death.

The sunrise over the Cascade Mountains was glorious, the light creeping up over the horizon, then spilling across his western-Washington vineyard like the promise it was. The morning sun was a reassurance, the pledge of another day, another opportunity. Mary had been the one to teach him that, but he'd never fully appreciated her enthusiasm for mornings until it was too late. He wished he'd shared more sunrises with his beloved wife.

Their only grandson now suffered from the same rare form of leukemia that had claimed her prematurely. It looked as if Tanner, too, would die. Matthias's jaw tensed and he closed his eyes. How could a loving God let an innocent child suffer like this?

What made an untenable situation even worse was the fact that his daughter bore the burden alone. Her ex had done nothing for her or the boy, making Matthias feel doubly responsible, but beyond phone calls and the occasional visit, there was little he could do to help her from where he lived.

The phone rang and Matthias hurried back to the house, hoping for good news. "Hello," he answered in his usual gruff voice.

"It's Harry."

A longtime friend and vineyard owner from the Napa Valley. "A little early for you to be phoning, don't you think?" Matthias couldn't prevent his disappointment from showing. He'd been hoping it was his daughter, Gloria, on the phone. He sighed heavily. It damn near killed Matthias that he was as powerless to help the boy as he'd been with Mary.

"I've got news that'll cheer you right up," Harry said.

"I could use some good news."

"It's about Greg Bennett."

Matthias stiffened at the sound of the name. He hated Greg Bennett with an intensity that had grown through the years. Bennett owed him. The success of the winery was largely due to Matthias's guiding hand. If it hadn't been for him, especially in those early years, Greg would have lost the vineyard ten times over.

The younger of the two Bennett boys had shown a talent for the business, but Matthias had been the one to teach him about grapes, about wine making, about operating an estate winery. Greg's father, John Bennett, had lived for the vineyard, to the point that it had destroyed his marriage. But he'd been impatient with the boy, an ineffective teacher.

A few years after Greg had joined Bennett Wines, John had died, and Greg had taken over. From that point on, Matthias had advised Greg, guided him and helped him expand enough to buy out his brother's share. Matthias had treated Greg as he would have treated his own son, if he'd had one. He'd shared everything with Greg Bennett, his skills and ideas, his enthusiasm for viticulture and wine making, his friendship. That was what made the betrayal so painful, so devastating. Mary's illness was an almost intolerable blow, but Greg's refusal to help them—that had been, in a way, an even greater blow.

Mary had loved Greg, too. Many nights she'd insisted Greg join them for dinner. She'd opened her home and her heart to Greg, and when she needed him, he'd said no. Neither bonds of family nor friendship, neither obligation nor gratitude, had influenced his decision.

"What about Greg?" Matthias asked now.

"He was in San Francisco looking for a loan."

So Greg's vineyard had been hit by fan leaf disease.

Matthias had suspected as much, but hadn't heard. "Did he get one?"

Harry paused for effect. "Not a dime."

"Good."

"I thought you'd like hearing that."

Matthias did, but not nearly as much as he'd hoped. All his energy was focused on doing what he could to help his daughter and grandson. For fifteen years his hatred of Greg Bennett had simmered, until it'd burned a hole straight through his heart. He couldn't forgive or forget, but his hatred no longer dominated every waking moment.

"You always said time wounds all heels."

Matthias grinned. Actually, Mary had been the one to say that.

"He's going to lose everything."

"It's what he deserves," Matthias said without emotion. The younger man had laid the foundation of his own troubles. If anything, Matthias was grateful he'd lived long enough to witness Bennett's downfall.

"I bet you think he should rot in hell," Harry said, and when Matthias didn't comment, his friend spoke again. "Hey, I hate the guy, too. Everyone does—although not as much as you do." He chuckled. "Well, I better get back to my morning coffee."

"Thanks for the call."

"Talk to you later," Harry said. A moment later, the line was disconnected.

Matthias appreciated knowing of Greg's financial problems. Fan leaf, a virus, had indiscriminately infected a number of vineyards in both the Sonoma and Napa valleys. Owners had been forced to tear out formerly productive vines and start anew, a prospect that was both time-consuming and expensive. Many of the small and medium-sized wineries in the two valleys were in danger of going under, Greg's included.

Mostly retired, Matthias needed something to occupy his time. In recent years he'd been working with local vineyard owners who were trying to grow vines resistant to the fan leaf virus before it had the same devastating results in Washington as in California.

Standing next to the phone, Matthias realized he should be dancing at the news about the disaster at Bennett Wines. A year ago, even six months ago, he would have been thrilled at the thought of Greg's troubles. Revenge was said to be a dish best eaten cold, and he'd certainly waited long enough to have it served to him. But he experienced damn little of the pleasure he'd anticipated. He'd wanted Greg to suffer the same agony that had tormented him as he stood by his wife's bedside.

The vineyard was everything to Greg, just as Matthias's only grandchild had become everything to him. And this time, they were both going to lose what they loved most.

"That is so sad," Mercy said, sitting on the edge of the counter in Matthias's kitchen. "Just look at him."

"He's worried sick about his grandson."

"What's going to happen to the boy?" Both Goodness and Mercy turned to Shirley.

"Do I look like I have a crystal ball?" Shirley asked irritably.

"I don't know about you two." Goodness reclined on the long counter. "But I was hoping for something a little less stressful during this visit to earth. We're assigned to a guy who's a real jerk. Someone who couldn't care less about anyone except himself."

"Yeah, but we're here on earth, aren't we?"

"Well, yes, but—"

"I agree with you," Shirley said, cutting in while the opportunity presented itself, "but we *can* help."

"Where's the fun? We got a human with his head so far up his—"

"Mercy!"

"A self-centered human," she revised. "You know, I think I'd feel better if Catherine had torn him to shreds. She should never have forgiven him."

"Mercy! Just listen to yourself."

"Right, right," she muttered, but Shirley could see that Greg was taking a toll on her friend's compassion.

"He's got too many problems for us to deal with," Goodness complained.

Shirley wasn't accustomed to such a defeatist attitude. "There's always his brother."

"What's this about a brother?" Goodness asked, suddenly attentive.

"Don't you remember?" Shirley did a double take. At their blank stares she sighed and reminded them.

"Phil. You remember reading about Philip Bennett, don't you? He's a big muck-a-muck with Pacific Union Bank. Greg considered going to him for a loan, but couldn't bring himself to do it."

"Why not?"

Shirley sighed again. It would help considerably if Goodness and Mercy had finished their research.

"Refresh my memory, would you?" Goodness asked.

Shirley felt the burden of responsibility. "You didn't read the whole file, did you?" she asked wearily.

"Ah . . . no."

"That's what I thought." It would do no good to lecture them now. "Greg's mother was dying while he was in the middle of his second divorce."

"I remember reading about Bobbi," Mercy said triumphantly. "His second trophy wife."

"His second attempt to find another Catherine, you mean," Goodness muttered.

"Yeah, yeah. What does Bobbi and their divorce have to do with Greg's mother?" Mercy asked. Both angels were lying on their stomachs now, chins propped on their hands.

"You didn't finish reading the file, either?" Shirley was dismayed.

Anything that was going to get accomplished on this mission would obviously be up to her.

"It was too depressing."

"I don't have the patience to cope with men like him," Goodness said.

"Go on about his mother," Mercy urged, motioning with her hand for Shirley to continue.

"Greg hid as much of his wealth as he could from Bobbi, mostly in stocks and bonds. Otherwise she'd want her share in a divorce settlement."

"Were they married long enough for her to get much?"

Like most angelic beings, neither Goodness nor Mercy fully understood the way such matters were handled on earth. "Didn't matter," Shirley said. "She had a good attorney."

"Oh." Apparently Goodness and Mercy were knowledgeable enough to know what that meant.

"Lydia Bennett was dying and asked to see Greg," Shirley continued. "Unfortunately her request came the morning of his settlement hearing. Greg chose to go to court. I'm sure that if he'd known his mother would die before he got to the hospital, he would've canceled the court date."

"Oh, my," Goodness whispered.

"Phil never forgave him?"

"Never. They haven't spoken in ten years."

Goodness sat up and looked around. "I don't know if I can take much more of this. You two do what you want, but I need a break."

"Where are you going?" Shirley demanded. If her fellow angel got into any mischief, *she'd* be the one held accountable. As usual.

"Outside," Goodness called over her shoulder.

Without a word, Mercy followed Goodness.

"Mercy!" Shirley shouted.

Flustered now, she raced after the pair and came to an abrupt halt when she saw the hot-air balloons. Their huge parachutes with the bright rainbow-colored panels brightened the sky. There must have been a dozen balloons in the lower Kent Valley. She knew that conditions in the early-morning hours were often ideal for ballooning.

"Goodness! Mercy! Don't even think—" She was too late. Shirley caught sight of them as they hopped into a wicker carriage already filled to capacity. The ground crew was about to release the giant balloon from its tether line.

"Goodness!" Shirley called, exasperated beyond measure. "Mercy! Get out of there!"

Both pretended not to hear her. Shirley had to be careful. It wasn't uncommon for humans, especially young ones between the ages of one and five, to hear angels speak. Some older people possessed the ability, too. Inside the basket was an eighty-year-old grandmother who was taking the flight as a birthday gift from her grandchildren.

"For the love of heaven, will you two kindly—" Shirley froze, certain she was seeing things. The hot-air balloon had risen only about six feet off the ground, where it remained, hovering, even though the ropes that had bound the craft to earth had been set free.

"What's happening?" the old woman called to the ground crew, who'd stepped aside, obviously waiting for the balloon to glide upward. "Shouldn't we be going up?"

Shirley groaned when she saw the problem. Just as she'd ordered, Goodness and Mercy had indeed left the wicker basket, but had taken positions outside it, securing the dangling tether lines to the ground.

"Let go," Shirley yelled.

"Are you sure that's what you really want us to do?" Goodness asked.

Without waiting for a response, both Goodness and Mercy released their tether lines at the same time. The balloon shot into the sky like a rocket. A few seconds later, its speed became more sedate.

"Wow!" Shirley heard the grandmother shout, holding on to her protective helmet with one hand and gripping the basket with the other. "Can we do that again?"

Goodness stood next to Shirley, looking extremely pleased with herself.

"That felt wonderful."

"You've risked the entire mission," Shirley said coldly. "Gabriel is sure to hear about this."

"Look at this," Mercy called as she joined them. She held a bottle of sparkling wine in one hand and dangled a trio of champagne flutes in the other.

"Where'd you get that?" Shirley asked.

"They fell from the sky." She grinned broadly as she said it.

"Come on, Shirl," Goodness cajoled, "humans aren't the only ones who enjoy a glass of bubbly now and then."

Five

Greg had barely slept or eaten in five days. He hadn't recognized the gaunt beleaguered man who'd stared back at him in the bathroom mirror that morning. For a long time he'd studied his reflection, shocked into numbness. Anyone seeing him would assume his condition was due to either the stress of his vineyard being wiped out or the failure of his third marriage. Neither was true.

He had a son. Catherine had given birth to a boy, raised that child, loved him, guided him into adulthood. Now this child, the son Greg had rejected, was a doctor. His son was a father himself, which made Greg a grandfather. A grandfather! That knowledge was heady stuff for a man who'd never . . . never been a real father and never would be. When he'd abandoned Catherine and the child, Greg had assumed there'd be plenty of time for a wife and family. He hadn't realized back then that this child of Catherine's was his only chance. In his cowardice he'd thrown away the very life he'd always expected to have.

The first emotion he'd felt when Catherine told him about Edward had been undiluted joy. He had no right to feel anything—he knew that without her having to say it but it'd been impossible to hide his reaction. Catherine always did possess the uncanny ability to see through him. It was one reason he hadn't been able to face her after she'd told him about the pregnancy.

Evading responsibility, he'd run and hadn't looked back—but he'd been looking back plenty these past five days. Every waking minute, to be precise.

Greg wouldn't have blamed Catherine if she'd ranted at him, called him every ugly name her vocabulary would allow. But she hadn't. Instead, she'd offered him a gracious forgiveness, of which he felt completely undeserving.

He could have accepted her anger far more easily than her generosity of spirit. As unbelievable as it seemed, *she* was the one who'd made excuses for the shabby way he'd treated her.

All Greg could do was torment himself by thinking of the opportunities he'd missed when he walked out on Catherine. Since their meeting Friday afternoon, the sick feeling in the pit of his stomach had refused to go away. He didn't know what to do next, but one thing was clear: he had to do *something*.

Catherine had said she'd get in touch with him about his meeting Edward. He could tell she wasn't keen on the idea; her pointed remark that Edward already had a father had hit its mark. She'd said the decision would come after she'd had a chance to talk it over with her husband, Larry, and with Edward himself. They'd parted then, with Catherine promising to call soon.

He hadn't heard from her since, and the waiting was killing him.

By five that evening Greg had lost patience and decided to call Catherine. He hurried into his office and reached for the telephone, intent on dialing directory assistance. As he lifted the receiver, a week's worth of mail slipped off his desk and onto the carpet.

With money pressures the way they were, Greg had been ignoring the mail, which consisted mainly of past-due notices and dunning letters from his attorneys. He stooped to pick up the envelopes, and that was when he saw it.

A letter addressed to him in Catherine's flowing penmanship. Thirty-five years, and he still recognized her beautiful handwriting.

Without conscious thought, he replaced the receiver. He studied the envelope carefully, noting the postmark. She'd mailed it the day after their meeting. He held it for a couple of minutes before he had the courage to open it.

The letter was brief.

Saturday, December 4

Dear Greg,

I'm sure you were as shocked to see me yesterday as I was to see you. As I said, I always thought we'd meet again one day, but I was still unprepared for actually running into you.

I should have anticipated that you'd want to meet the son you fathered. It was short-sighted of me not to consider that before. I discussed it with Larry. My husband is both wise and generous, and he felt neither of us should be involved in making such an important decision. He thought

I should leave it entirely up to Edward.

I was able to reach Edward yesterday evening. It wasn't an easy conversation. He had a number of questions—ones I'd been able to avoid until now. I answered him truthfully; perhaps because I did, he's decided against meeting you.

I'm sorry, Greg. I know this disappoints you.

Catherine

Greg read the letter a second time, then slumped in his chair, eyes closed, while sharp pangs of disappointment stabbed him. It didn't escape his notice that Catherine had used the same form of communication he'd used when he deserted her. When he'd seen her the previous week, he'd given her his business card with his personal phone number. She could have put him out of his agony days earlier; instead, she'd chosen to torment him. She'd probably derived a great deal of satisfaction from turning him down, letting him know he wasn't wanted. No doubt, she'd waited thirty-five years for the privilege.

In an outburst of anger he crumpled the letter and tossed it in the wastebasket. Still not satisfied, he swept his arm across the desktop, knocking everything onto the carpet. His chest heaving, he buried his face in both hands.

The Christmas spirit had infected Phil Bennett. He hummed along to "Silent Night," which played on the bedroom radio, as he changed out of his business suit on Wednesday evening. Some people liked secular Christmas music the best, but Phil preferred the carols.

"You certainly seem to be in a good mood this evening," his wife remarked when he joined her in the kitchen for dinner. Sandy had grown a little thick through the waist over the past decade, but then, so had he. They'd been married for more than thirty years and raised three daughters and now they were both looking forward to retiring. The previous year, Phil and Sandy had purchased property in Arizona and planned to build in a retirement community, together with their best friends. It wouldn't be long now before the only real commuting he'd do would be on a par-three golf course.

"What makes you so happy?" Sandy asked as she brought a platter of meat loaf to the small kitchen table. With the children grown and on their own, Phil and Sandy had taken to eating their meals in the kitchen, instead of the dining room.

"I don't know," Phil said, carrying over the tossed green salad. When she wasn't looking, he removed a sliced cucumber and munched on it.

"Well, then, I'm glad to see you've got the spirit of the season," Sandy said absently as she placed a bowl of steaming scalloped potatoes on a trivet.

"I do indeed," Phil murmured, even though it wasn't Christmas that had made him so cheerful. Actually, Christmas had very little to do with it, but he wasn't telling his wife that.

Once Sandy found out that his glee was entirely because of what he'd learned about his brother's financial woes, she was sure to lecture him. And Phil was in too fine a mood to be chastised.

Word had reached him that afternoon of Greg's numerous attempts to obtain financing for Bennett Wines. It did his heart good to learn that his ungrateful arrogant younger brother was about to receive the justice he so amply deserved.

"You're going to choir practice tonight, aren't you?" Sandy asked as she pulled out the chair across from him and sat down.

Caught up in his own thoughts, Phil didn't hear her right away. "Choir practice?" he repeated as he helped himself to a warm-from-the-oven biscuit.

"Phil!"

"Of course I'm going."

She relaxed. "Good. We need all the practice we can get."

Phil had recently joined the choir. It was his way of being part of the church community and contributing to the service.

So far, he knew only a few of the other choir members by name, but he'd know them all soon enough, especially now that they were meeting three nights a week to prepare for the Christmas cantata.

Unlike his brother, Phil was personable and generous—if he did say so himself. Plus, he had a reasonably pleasant singing voice. Greg didn't. Oh, his younger brother had certain talents, no question. He'd made Bennett Wines a respected label, well-known to wine cognoscenti. He had a single-minded focus that had led to his success. He could be charming when it was to his advantage.

And he was a ruthless bastard.

Phil had been waiting years for his brother to get what was coming to him. Years. The troubles currently plaguing California's wine industry had dominated the local news channels for weeks. Fan leaf virus was causing the ruin of many vineyards, and of course, Phil had wondered about Greg. But he hadn't heard anything definite until that very day. What he'd learned made him eager to sing.

After all these years, it was payback time. Greg had deserted a woman in need; Phil hadn't known Catherine well, but he'd liked her . . . and he'd heard rumors about a pregnancy. Then, perhaps worst of all, Greg had ignored his own mother on her deathbed, and when Phil had confronted him, he hadn't shown any genuine remorse.

Naturally, because of his religious beliefs, Phil tried not to hate his brother. He was willing to admit, though, that he felt strongly antagonistic toward Greg, not to mention gleeful about his financial woes.

He hadn't missed the fact that the one place Greg hadn't come to apply for a loan was Pacific Union. A wise decision. Given the opportunity, Phil would have relished personally refusing his brother's application. More than that, he'd done everything he could to make sure Greg didn't obtain funding. Actually, he'd handled that situation in a pretty clever way. He'd sent word through the banking community that when an application came to them from Bennett Wines, no one was to accept it. He'd given the impression that he'd be the one helping his brother.

If Sandy learned about this, she'd be furious. She'd accuse him of sabotaging Greg's business, but that wasn't how Phil viewed it. All he'd done was make sure Greg didn't get anything he didn't deserve. It'd probably be the first time, too. From childhood on, Greg had been the favored son. His fascination with that damned vineyard had guaranteed his special position with their father. And perhaps because he was the youngest, Greg had been coddled by their mother.

Even when she was dying, she'd made excuses for him. It was now ten years since they'd buried their mother, and every time Phil thought about the funeral, the fury he still felt toward his brother threatened to consume him.

The grief Greg had shown was as phoney as a three-dollar bill. If he'd cared even a little about their mother, he would have come to the hospital when she asked for him. They'd known her illness was terminal! Nothing could have been more important; nothing should have kept him away. When Phil found out that Greg had chosen to attend the settlement hearing on his divorce case instead, he'd completely lost his temper.

The two brothers had nearly come to blows at the wake. What irked Phil the most was the grieving-son act Greg had put on for family and friends.

Grieving? Yeah, right.

Phil had been appalled by the number of people who seemed to fall for Greg's act. Phil had been hurting, too, but he'd disciplined himself not to show his emotions. Grief was private, after all. He'd also grown accustomed to the reality of her death, because he'd been there. His mother's illness had lasted several months, and Phil had been the one to sit at her bedside, to read to her and comfort her.

Sure, his brother had come to visit on occasion, but he always had a convenient excuse for not staying long. In the beginning it was because he was harvesting the grapes. That was followed by the wine-production period, which he said demanded constant supervision. During the last months of their mother's life, Greg had been involved in his divorce, too. His *second* divorce.

As far as Phil was concerned, his brother's marital problems were exactly what he deserved. The first wife, who'd lasted ten years, was bad enough. The second one, who looked shockingly like the first, had stayed around three years, possibly four, he couldn't remember. Phil had heard that there was a third Mrs. Greg Bennett, and he couldn't help wondering if she'd go the way of her predecessors.

"Phil, hurry, or we're going to be late," Sandy called from the kitchen.

They'd finished dinner and washed their few dishes, and while Sandy was collecting the sheet music, Phil watched the last of the national news.

“I’m ready,” he called back, turning off the TV. Preoccupied with thoughts of his brother, Phil hadn’t heard a word of the newscast.

The church parking lot was only partially filled when they arrived. The choir director smiled in greeting, but didn’t allow anyone to waste time. The Christmas cantata was only two weeks away, and there remained plenty of room for improvement.

The choir members gathered on the bleachers; as a tenor, Phil stood in the back row behind the women singing first soprano. It wasn’t until they started the first song that he noticed the blonde standing directly in front of him. He’d never heard anyone with a more spectacular voice. It was hard to remember his own part. The woman’s clear strong voice was so stunning he was completely distracted.

“I don’t believe we’ve met,” he said during the break.

She turned around and smiled. “We haven’t.”

“Phil Bennett,” he said.

“I know.”

“You do?”

“Oh, yes. I know quite a bit about you, Mr. Bennett.”

This was something. Phil squared his shoulders a bit, feeling downright flattered by this lovely woman’s interest.

The director was pleased with their performance and after an hour and a half, dismissed them for the night.

“We sounded quite good, didn’t we?” Sandy said on the drive home.

"I thought so, too. By the way, who was the woman standing in front of me?"

"Mrs. Hansen?"

"No, the blonde."

His wife cast him a curious look. "There wasn't any blonde standing in front of you."

"Yes, there was. We spoke. You couldn't have missed her, Sandy. She had the most angelic voice. Really gifted."

Sandy laughed softly. "And what was her name?"

Phil hesitated, trying to remember. "I don't believe she gave it to me."

"I see." Although Sandy wasn't actually smiling, he heard the amusement in her voice.

"I'm telling you there was a blond woman standing in front of me, and she sang like no one I've ever heard."

"If you say so, darling."

Women! If Sandy hadn't seen the blonde for herself, Phil couldn't make her believe she'd been there. Next practice, he'd be sure to introduce the woman to his wife. Then he'd see what Sandy had to say.

Six

"Goodness!" Shirley waited until the church had emptied before chastising her fellow angel. She just didn't know how to handle Goodness and Mercy. Their antics were going to get them permanently expelled from earth. "You had to do it, didn't you?"

At least Goodness had the decency to look properly

repentant. "You're right, I know you're right, but I couldn't stand the smug way Phil Bennett was acting. From the moment he heard about his brother's problems, he was beside himself with pleasure. All his talk about being a good Christian, too!"

"We aren't here to deal with Phil Bennett."

"But he's part and parcel of what's happening to Greg."

"Well, yes, and no . . ."

"I don't think we need to worry," Mercy told her. "If Gabriel's going to be upset with us, it'll be because of what happened with the hot-air balloon. Goodness singing in a church choir is minor compared to that."

Shirley had done her utmost to put the balloon episode out of her mind, and Mercy's reference did nothing to calm her already tattered nerves. "Please, don't remind me."

"If Gabriel didn't hear about *that,* then we don't need to—" Mercy stopped midsentence. A panic-stricken look came over her face, and she blinked several times before she said, "Oh . . . hello, Gabriel."

"Hello, Gabriel," Goodness repeated, wide-eyed and subservient.

"The Archangel Gabriel to you," their boss said sternly.

Feeling slightly light-headed, Shirley turned around and swallowed nervously. She opened her mouth to offer a multitude of excuses and saw that it would do no good. Their chances of putting something over on the archangel were virtually nil.

"I'm here for a progress report," he announced in the same controlled voice.

Goodness and Mercy both gazed pleadingly at Shirley, silently begging her to respond. She glared at them. When she tried to speak, her tongue seemed glued to the roof of her mouth.

"Well?" Gabriel muttered. "I'm waiting."

"Greg talked to Catherine and he knows he fathered a son," Shirley blurted out.

"Are you telling me that after thirty-five years, Greg just *happened* to stumble upon Catherine?" Gabriel demanded.

Shirley was never sure how much Gabriel knew of their antics, but suspected he was aware of it all. The questions were most likely a test to see how much they'd learned. . . .

All three nodded in unison.

The archangel's frown darkened. "Thanks to a tableful of spilled crab, as I understand it."

"Yes, but that was only a means—"

"To an end," Gabriel completed for Mercy.

"Yes, and it worked very nicely, in my humble opinion," Goodness said in a bold rush. "It seemed a shame for the two of them to be in the same place after all those years and not know it. Really, all I did was point Greg out to Catherine. It was up to her to ignore or confront him."

"Yes," Mercy agreed. "Greg never did appreciate Catherine's strength."

"In other words, you're telling me," Gabriel said

thoughtfully, "that Catherine chose to face him?"

Again all three nodded as one.

Gabriel's smile seemed involuntary. "The truth is, Catherine has Greg to thank for that inner strength. She gained it when he deserted her."

"They might never have met again if it hadn't been for those spilled crabs." Goodness made her foolishness sound like an act of genius.

Gabriel didn't look pleased—nor should he, Shirley reasoned. But that one antic *had* worked beautifully. She'd admit it now, even though she hadn't approved at the time.

"Do you have anything else to report?" Gabriel asked.

The three glanced at one another and shrugged.

"We've been to visit Matthias in the Seattle area," Mercy told him in an offhand manner meant to suggest that Gabriel probably already knew about it. "He still hates Greg, but he's more concerned about his grandson's condition just now."

"Ah, yes," Gabriel said, frowning again. "I've heard something about that. Cancer, is it?"

Shirley nodded. "The same form of leukemia that killed the boy's grandmother." Then, because she wanted to impress upon the archangel that their time on earth had been well spent, she said, "We've been to see Greg's brother, as well. Phil Bennett. You remember him, don't you?"

"Of course," Gabriel assured them. "I didn't realize Goodness enjoyed singing in choirs as much as she does. I'm sure she'll volunteer to be part of the heavenly host next year—is that correct?"

"Ah . . ." Goodness waited desperately for Shirley to rescue her, but Shirley was in no mood to offer assistance. She might have leaped in to save her friend, if not for that escapade with the hot-air balloon. She felt mortified every time she thought about it. True, the sparkling wine had gone a long way toward tempering her anger, but . . .

"I'll be happy to serve wherever assigned," Goodness stated with a woeful look in Shirley's direction.

Gabriel arched his brows as if to say her willingness surprised him. "I find your attitude a refreshing change from when we last spoke."

"Singing with the heavenly host isn't my favorite Christmas duty," Goodness was quick to add, "but I'll serve wherever you feel I'd do best."

Once again Gabriel's expression implied that he was having trouble believing her. "Anything else you'd like to report?" he finally asked.

"Not a thing," Shirley said, eager for him to be on his way.

"None."

"Nothing I can think of."

He stared at the three of them. "All right, then, carry on. Just remember there are less than three weeks until Christmas."

"Oh, yes," they said in unison. They'd made a lucky escape, Shirley felt. Gabriel hadn't even mentioned the hot-air balloon.

"It was very good of you to check up on us," Goodness said.

That was overdoing it, in Shirley's opinion. She resisted the urge to step on the other angel's foot.

"Oh, yes," Mercy chimed in. "Stop by again any time." For good measure, she added a small wave.

Shirley sent both Goodness and Mercy looks potent enough to perm their hair.

Gabriel turned away, then abruptly turned back. "I had no idea you three enjoyed wine."

Not one of them uttered a word. Shirley swallowed hard, certain they were going to be plucking harp strings on some cloud for the remainder of their careers.

"I don't suppose you happened to notice the label, did you?" he asked.

No one answered.

"That's what I thought," Gabriel said. "It was the Bennett label. Greg Bennett is a talented wine maker. It would be a pity for him to go out of business, don't you think?" Not giving them the opportunity to respond, Gabriel whisked back to the realms of glory.

Greg Bennett had an aversion to the antiseptic smell that permeated hospitals. It nearly overpowered him the minute he walked through the large glass doors of San Francisco General. His dislike of hospitals was linked to his mother's long stay before her death, he supposed. That, and his own revulsion to needles and blood.

He paused at the information center.

"Can I help you?" a much-too-perky candy striper asked him.

"Where might I find Dr. Edward Thorpe?"

"Oh, you're here about the article. That's wonderful!"

Article? What article? Greg hadn't a clue, but he played along as if he did. His son had decided he didn't want to meet him, and that was his choice, but Greg wanted to see Edward. *Needed* to see him. He wasn't going to make an issue of it, wasn't going to announce who he was. He didn't plan to cause a scene or even call attention to himself. It was just that his curiosity had gotten the better of him. . . .

Greg realized he'd given up his parental rights years ago, but he couldn't leave matters as they were. Not now that he knew Catherine had borne the child.

Catherine had mentioned the physical resemblance between them, and Greg felt an urge to simply see his son. He doubted they'd exchange a word. Without ever knowing him, without *wanting* to know him, Edward had rejected Greg.

Like father, like son.

"Take the elevator to the fifth floor." The young woman at the information desk pointed toward the row of elevators on the opposite side of the lobby. "Tell the nurse at the desk that you're here for the blood test."

"Ah." Greg hesitated. Did she say *blood?* He was most definitely not interested in anything to do with blood.

"I think it's wonderful of you," she added with a sweetness that made him want to cringe.

Greg didn't feel wonderful. Furthermore, he had no intention of giving anyone a drop of his blood. Not without one hell of a fight first.

"Dr. Edward Thorpe—you're sure he's there?"

"He's on the fifth floor," the woman assured him. "Just ask for him at the nurses' station."

"Thank you," he said, turning toward the bank of elevators.

"No, thank *you,*" she called after him.

Greg got off the elevator at the fifth floor and to his surprise walked into a corridor filled with people. As instructed, he headed for the nurses' station, but before he could say a word, he was handed a clipboard.

"Complete the form, sign the bottom of the page and bring this back to me when you're finished."

Greg stared at the woman. "What's it for?"

"We need you to fill out the questionnaire and sign the release if we're going to take your blood." Unlike the perky candy striper, this one looked harassed and overworked.

"I realize that, but—"

"Just read the form. If you have any questions after that, I'll be happy to answer them."

That sounded fair enough. Greg joined the others, sat down and read the page. It was exactly what the nurse had said. Basically, San Francisco General was requesting permission to draw blood. Not that he'd give it. Not in this lifetime.

As soon as he finished reading the form, he knew it was time to leave. He was about to pick himself up and discreetly disappear when a physician entered the room.

Conversation stopped as the man stood before the group and started to speak. Greg glanced up and froze. It was Edward. He recognized him immediately, long before he looked at the identification badge that hung around his neck.

"Has everyone finished signing the waiver?" Dr. Thorpe asked. "If you've decided this isn't something that interests you, you can leave now. We appreciate your time. For those of you who wish to continue, we promise to make this as quick and painless as possible. Before you know it, you'll be on your way."

Three or four people left the room.

Greg could follow them or proceed with this. Swallowing his natural aversion, he quickly signed his name. Okay, so he had to give a little of his blood. No big deal. He'd give a lot more if it meant he could spend a few minutes getting to know his son.

Catherine was right about one thing. Edward was tall and distinguished-looking, but as far as family resemblance went, Greg didn't see it. Still, he couldn't stop staring. This was *his* son. Edward looked good. Damn good. One glance had told Greg that his son was everything he wasn't. Dedicated. Compassionate. Smart.

"I'll need that," the nurse said as Greg shuffled past.

He gave her the clipboard and walked down the corridor, along with the others.

"Before we go any farther," Edward said, "I want to personally thank each of you for your generous response to the recent newspaper article. We didn't have this many volunteers in the entire month of November. I'd like to think the Christmas spirit has touched us all. Does anyone have any questions?"

A man with prematurely white hair raised his hand. "What will happen if we're a match?"

While Edward talked about obscure-sounding medical procedures, Greg leaned toward the woman standing ahead of him. "A match for what?"

"Bone marrow," she muttered out of the corner of her mouth, then turned to eye him. "Are you sure you're supposed to be here?"

If ever a question needed answering, this was it.

"No," he said more to himself than to her. He wasn't sure of anything. Curiosity had brought him to the hospital. A curiosity so deep it had consumed him for days. After thirty-five years of not knowing, not caring, he now felt an overwhelming desire to see his son.

"Who'd like to go first?"

Before Greg could stop himself, he shot his hand into the air.

"Great. Follow me." Greg stepped out of the line and followed his son down the corridor to a cubicle.

"The nurse will be right in to draw blood."

"Aren't you going to take it yourself?" Greg asked. Already he could feel his panic level rise.

Edward shrugged lightly. "Well . . . the nurse usually does this."

“I’d prefer if you did it yourself. In fact, I insist on it.”

Surprise showing in his eyes, Edward turned to face him. It seemed he was about to refuse, but for reasons Greg wouldn’t question, silently led him to a chair and instructed him to sit down.

Greg sat, unbuttoned his shirtsleeve and rolled it up.

“Do I know you?” Edward asked, studying him carefully.

“No,” Greg responded. “Do I remind you of anyone?” He was well aware that this was an unfair question.

“No, but I thought you might be a friend of my father’s, Dr. Larry Thorpe.”

“No, I’ve never met him.”

Edward took a short piece of what looked like rubber tubing and tied it around Greg’s upper arm. Next he gingerly tested the skin. “Nice blood vessels. We shouldn’t have any problem.”

“Good.” Greg’s mouth went dry at the sight of the needle, and closing his eyes, he looked away. This was even worse than the last time he’d had blood tests. He felt the needle against his skin and braced himself for the small prick of pain. As a kid he’d fainted in the doctor’s office every time he received a shot or had blood drawn; he wasn’t keen to relive the experience. That was years ago, but even now, as an adult, he generally avoided annual checkups if he could and— The needle was the last thing he noticed until he heard Edward’s voice, which seemed to boom at him like a foghorn.

"Are you awake?"

Greg blinked and realized he was lying on the floor. Edward knelt beside him.

Their eyes met, and embarrassed, Greg glanced away. "What happened?" he asked, still in a daze.

"You passed out."

"I did?" Abruptly Greg sat upright. He would have fled, but the room had started to swim in the most disturbing fashion.

"Take it slowly," Edward advised, then helped him stand up. "I've asked one of the nurses to take your blood pressure. Tell me, when was the last time you had anything to eat?"

"I'm fine. I had breakfast this morning." It was a lie. He wasn't fine and he hadn't eaten breakfast. "I just don't happen to like needles."

"Then it's a brave thing you did, coming in here like this."

"Brave?" Greg repeated with a short laugh. "I'm the biggest coward who ever lived."

Seven

On Monday morning Greg recognized that he had no other options left to him. It wouldn't be easy to apply for a loan at Pacific Union Bank, but he had nowhere else to go. He'd never been a person to beg. Never *needed* to beg until now, but if begging would help him hold on to Bennett Wines, he'd do that and more.

The worst of it was that he'd have to go begging to

his own brother. Phil, who'd like nothing better than to call him a failure. He wouldn't be far from wrong; Greg *felt* like a failure.

Despite his mood, Greg prepared carefully for the interview, wearing his best suit. He was about to head out the door when his phone rang. Caller ID told him it wasn't a creditor.

"Hello," he snapped.

"Hello, Greg."

It was Tess, his almost ex-wife. Ex-wife number three. "What's the matter? Are you after another pound of flesh?" he sneered. The last thing he needed right now was to deal with spoiled selfish Tess.

"I heard about your money problems."

"I'll bet you're gloating, too."

He heard her intake of breath. "I don't wish you ill, Greg."

He didn't believe her for a moment. "What do you want?" He was facing an unpleasant task that demanded all his attention, and he didn't want to be waylaid by an even more unpleasant one.

"I called because I didn't realize the extent of your money problems until now and, well . . . I'm sorry."

He said nothing.

"I wish you'd told me earlier. If I'd known, perhaps—"

"Would it have made any difference?" Their troubles had started long before the fan leaf virus had destroyed his vines. Long before he'd been confronted with one financial crisis after another. He knew when he and Tess got married that they were probably making a mistake. Still, that hadn't stopped him. He'd wanted her, and she'd wanted the prestige of being married to him. True, they looked good together, but at the moment it seemed that was *all* they'd had going for them.

He didn't like living alone, but he figured he'd get used to it eventually.

She didn't answer his probing question right away. "If I'd known about your troubles, I like to think it would have changed things."

All women preferred to believe the best about themselves, he thought cynically. "Think what you like," he muttered.

"Oh, Greg, do you hate me that much?"

Her words caught him up short. "I don't hate you at all," he said, and realized it was true. He was sorry to see the marriage end, but he hadn't been surprised and, in fact, had anticipated their divorce long before Tess moved out.

"You don't?" She sounded surprised, but recovered quickly. "Good, because I was thinking we should both do away with these attorneys and settle matters on our own. I can't afford three-hundred dollars an hour, and neither can you."

Greg wasn't sure he should put too much faith in this sudden change of heart. "Do you mean it?"

"Of course I do."

"All right, name a date and a time, and I'll be there." Greg hated the eagerness that crept into his voice, but he wanted the attorneys out of these divorce proceedings as much as Tess did. Without them—stirring up animosities, asking for unreasonable concessions—he and Tess had a chance of making this separation amicable.

"How about next Tuesday night?" she suggested.

Greg noted the time and place and, with a farewell that verged on friendly, they ended the call.

Well, well. Life was full of surprises, and not all of them unpleasant.

The drive into the city, however, could only be called unpleasant. Traffic was heavy and Greg soon lost his patience, particularly when it took him nearly an hour to find parking, and that wasn't even close to the financial district. The cost of parking in San Francisco should be illegal, he grumbled to himself. This was his third trip into the city within ten days; he hadn't been to San Francisco three times in the entire previous year. Greg preferred his role as lord of the manor—a role that was about to be permanently canceled if he couldn't secure a loan.

The sidewalks were crowded, since it was almost lunchtime. A brisk wind blew off the bay and he hunched his shoulders against it, ignoring the expensive-looking decorations on the bank buildings and the tasteful Christmas music floating out from well-appointed lobbies as doors were opened.

He sincerely hoped he wouldn't be forced to see Phil this early in the process, if at all. Knowing Phil as he did, Greg was keenly aware that his brother would take real pleasure in personally rejecting his application. Then again, he might exercise some modicum of mercy and leave it to someone else, a junior officer. But that wasn't something Greg needed to worry about just yet. Today was only the first step—meeting with a loan officer and completing the lengthy application. Once he'd finished the paperwork, he could leave. Walk out the doors of yet another bank, wait for yet another rejection.

He hated his own pessimistic attitude, but nothing had happened in the past week to give him any hope. His brother hated him—it was that simple—and Phil wasn't the kind of man to put their argument behind him. If he hadn't forgiven Greg in ten years, he wasn't likely to do it now.

Phil had always been somewhat jealous of him, Greg knew, something he'd never really understood. Greg supposed his greatest sin was the fact that he'd been born last. That, and sharing a passion for wine making with his father. Despite what Phil believed, Greg had loved their mother. Her death, although expected, had hit him hard.

He'd had no way of knowing how critical her condition was. They'd spoken briefly the night before, and while she'd sounded weak, she'd encouraged him to take care of his own business, to keep his appointment at court. So he'd felt there was still plenty of time. She hadn't seemed that close to death.

His fight with Phil after the funeral had been the

lowest point in his life. The truth was, Phil hadn't called him any name he hadn't called himself in the years since.

When Greg had finished with the loan application at Pacific Union, he walked back to the parking lot and paid the attendant what amounted to a ransom. But instead of heading for the St. Francis for a good stiff drink as was his custom, Greg drove to Viewcrest, the cemetery where his mother was buried.

He spent more than an hour wandering down long grassy rows in the biting wind before he located his mother's grave. He stood there, gazing down at the marker. *Lydia Smith Bennett, 1930-1989 Beloved Mother.* Phil had arranged for that stone. Phil had made all the arrangements.

This was Greg's first visit since they'd buried her. He shook his head, brushing away tears,overwhelmed by all the things he'd left unsaid. *I loved you, Mom. I did. I do. I'm sorry . . .*

Eventually he squatted down, touched his fingers to his lips and pressed them to the marble gravestone. A long moment passed before he stood up again, shoulders bent, head bowed, and silently walked away.

"Has anyone got a tissue?" Mercy wailed, and when no one responded, she threw herself against Goodness, wiping her face on her friend's soft sleeve.

"Would you kindly *stop?*"

But Goodness sounded suspiciously tearful. Shirley,

too, was having a hard time holding back her emotions. Seeing Greg like this, broken and defeated, was painful. She barely recognized him anymore. She didn't know when it had happened or how, but she'd started to care about this man. Obviously Goodness and Mercy had also revised their feelings toward him.

"We've got to do something to help Greg!"

"We're trying," Shirley said.

"But he's in bad shape."

"I have a feeling it's going to get worse," Shirley whispered, fearing the future.

"Say it isn't so." Mercy wailed all the louder.

"His brother's going to reject the loan, isn't he?"

Shirley couldn't imagine Phil making any other decision and said as much.

"Not if I have anything to say about it," Goodness cried. "I think it's time I got ready for choir practice again, don't you?"

"Goodness, no!"

"I don't care if Gabriel sends me back to singing with the heavenly host or even gate-keeping. Phil Bennett is about to get a piece of my mind."

"Goodness," Mercy gasped.

"What?"

"Goodness," Shirley began. "You—"

"I'm going, too." Mercy glanced at Shirley.

Shirley could see she had no choice. "Oh, all right, but we can't all three join the choir."

"Why not?" Mercy asked, rushing to catch up with Goodness.

Shirley shook her head in wonder, sure they'd be facing the wrath of Gabriel once again. She just hoped the sacrifice they were prepared to make on Greg Bennett's behalf would turn out to be worth it.

"Phil, I swear you haven't heard a word I've said all evening."

Phil lowered the evening newspaper and looked at his wife. "What gives you that impression?"

Sandy threw back her head with a frustrated groan and returned to the kitchen.

Reluctantly Phil followed her. He should have known better than to try bluffing his way out of this. After all these years of marriage, there wasn't much he could hide from Sandy. He was preoccupied, true. It had to do with his brother. His shiftless irresponsible no-good brother who'd once been everyone's golden boy. Well, not anymore.

"Greg was in the bank this afternoon," Phil told Sandy in a nonchalant voice, pouring himself a cup of coffee.

He had Sandy's full attention now. "Did you talk to him?" She knew as well as he did that they hadn't spoken since their mother's funeral.

"No-o-o." He shrugged and tried to look regretful. "Dave Hilaire was the one who dealt with him."

"Greg's applying for a loan?"

Phil replied with a somber nod, but he felt like jumping up and clicking his heels.

"I've been reading for weeks about the problems the

wineries have been experiencing," Sandy said thoughtfully. "It must be terrible to have some virus wipe out generations of work. From what I read, some vineyards were more badly hurt than others."

"Greg's vineyard is one of the worst hit," Phil explained in the same grave voice.

"I wondered about Bennett Wines. . . ."

"Me, too." He did his best to sound sympathetic.

Sandy studied him, her eyes narrowed, and Phil struggled to hide his true sentiments. This virus, or something like it, was exactly what he'd been waiting for. *Justice. Retribution. Revenge. Call it what you will.* Phil had suspected that sometime or other, Greg would come crawling to him, asking for help. He'd anticipated that day, longed for it.

"Are you going to be able to get him the loan?"

"I . . . I don't know," Phil hedged. He could hardly admit that he'd wear thong underwear in public before he'd sign off on the money Greg needed.

"But you'll do what you can?" Sandy gave him a hard look, and it was all he could do to meet her eyes.

"Of course," he said, sounding as sincere as he could.

She sighed, then walked over to him and kissed him on the cheek. "Good. I've always hoped you two would put aside your differences."

Phil hugged her rather than look her in the face. "I know."

"You're all Greg has in the way of close family."

True, but that hadn't made any difference to his

brother, and Phil didn't see why it should to him. Greg would come to him when he needed help and only because he needed help. So, any apology, any effort toward reconciliation, was tainted as far as Phil was concerned. Not that he intended to forgive his brother or had any interest in reconciling with him. It was too late for that. A just God would surely understand that some things were unforgivable. Wouldn't He?

"Poor Greg," Sandy whispered.

Oh, yes, and Greg wouldn't know how truly poor he was until Phil had finished with him.

"No wonder you weren't listening earlier," Sandy said, freeing herself from his embrace. "You had other things on your mind."

"I'm sorry, honey."

"You *are* going to help him, right?" Sandy was obviously seeking reassurance.

He nodded, still without looking at her.

"Fine. You'll be busy with that, so let's skip the practice. I'll tell Evelyn we can't do it."

Evelyn was the choir director. "Can't do what?"

"Go caroling Christmas Eve."

"Just a minute," Phil said. "Why not? We don't have anything on the schedule, do we? None of the girls can come until Christmas morning."

"You're sure you still want to?" Sandy asked, sounding pleased.

"Very sure."

"You're just hoping to see that blonde again, aren't you?" she teased.

The blonde he'd spoken with earlier in the week hadn't shown up for practice the last two times, and Phil was growing discouraged. She hadn't been a figment of his imagination, despite what Sandy claimed.

"Maybe I did just imagine her," he said to appease Sandy. "I have to keep you on your toes, don't I?"

"We're going to be singing at the hospital Christmas Eve. San Francisco General." Sandy eyed him as though expecting Phil to change his mind.

"That's all right." Not exactly his favorite place, but he could live with it.

Besides, singing carols for the sick was what Christmas was all about. This was the season of love and goodwill, and he had an abundant supply. Not for his brother, but that was Greg's own fault. "As a man sows, so shall he reap." That was somewhere in the Bible, and if anyone questioned his actions, Phil would happily quote it.

Oh, yes, his brother was getting exactly what he deserved.

Eight

Matthias stepped off the plane and walked through the long jetway to the terminal at San Francisco International Airport. He'd come to spend Christmas with his grandson, fearing it would be the boy's last.

He spotted his daughter in the crowd and rushed toward her. "Gloria," he whispered, hugging her close. She'd lost weight and looked pale and fragile.

This was destroying her—to watch her son dying, one day at a time. Matthias remembered how emotionally drained he'd become when Mary had been so terribly ill. Gloria had suffered then, too—and now she had to go through all this grief and pain again. . . . How could she bear it?

"Oh, Daddy, I have wonderful news!" his daughter exclaimed. "A donor's been found."

The unexpected relief, the gratitude Matthias suddenly felt made him go weak. "Where?" he asked hoarsely. "Who is it?"

"I don't know his name. He's a stranger, someone who responded to the article in last week's newspaper about the need for volunteers. Dr. Thorpe says he's making the phone call this afternoon and the whole process should start before Christmas. Isn't that *wonderful?* Oh, Daddy, I can't tell you how happy I am!"

"It's the best Christmas gift anyone could have given me."

"Me, too." Gloria's eyes shone with unshed tears. "Dr. Thorpe says the match is an especially good one. He sounded really hopeful, Dad. He didn't come right out and tell me this was going to save Tanner's life, but it is, I know it is. My heart tells me everything's going to be all right now." No longer did she struggle to hold back the tears. They fell unrestrained down her cheeks.

"When can I see this grandson of mine?" Matthias asked, eager now to reach the hospital.

They chatted nonstop on the drive into the city.

When they got to the hospital, they hurried to the eighth floor. Weak as he was, ten-year-old Tanner was sitting up in bed waiting for Matthias.

"Merry Christmas, Grandpa." His pale face was wreathed in an extra-wide grin, although his eyes were sunken and shadowed.

"Merry Christmas, Tanner." Matthias hugged his grandson, careful not to hurt the fragile little body. Seeing him like this was hard. So hard.

"Grandpa, are you crying?"

"It's only because I'm happy." Matthias glanced up and smiled apologetically at his daughter and the young nurse who stood beside her.

"Everything's going to be all right now," Gloria assured him again, and Matthias believed her. Everything *was* going to be better.

"Hello," Greg snapped into the small cellular phone. He'd never enjoyed talking on the telephone and was particularly annoyed by these new-fangled cell things.

"Is this Greg Bennett?"

"Yes." Again his voice was as sharp and short-tempered as he could make it. He was walking between the rows of dead and dying grapevines, recognizing with final certainty that nothing was salvageable. No one could save what had taken fifty years to build.

"This is Dr. Edward Thorpe from San Francisco General."

Greg was so shocked he nearly dropped the phone. "Yes . . . Dr. Thorpe."

"I was wondering if you'd be willing to come back to the hospital later this afternoon?" His voice was pleasant, smooth, and if Greg wasn't mistaken, there was a hint of relief, too.

"I'll be there," Greg told him immediately.

"I realize it's short notice and this is the Christmas season, but—"

"I'll be there," Greg interrupted. "What time?"

"Is three o'clock convenient?"

"Sure." Then he couldn't resist asking, "Can you tell me what this is about?"

"I'd prefer we discuss it once you get here." He ended the conversation by giving Greg detailed instructions on where and how to reach him at the hospital.

"I'll see you at three," Greg said, then slipped the phone back into his shirt pocket. He drew in a deep breath, releasing it slowly.

Somehow, some way, Edward had discovered the truth about their relationship. Apparently his son had experienced a change of heart and decided to meet his biological father, after all.

Although Greg could offer no excuse for what he'd done to Catherine, he was grateful for Edward's decision. He did want Edward to know that he was proud to have fathered him, proud of the man he'd become. Greg could claim no credit; Edward owed him nothing. He only hoped that one day his son would be able to forgive him. He'd like a relationship with him, but wouldn't ask. That, like everything else, was up to Edward.

The drive into the city was becoming almost routine by now. Greg found he was nervous and at the same time excited. He parked where Edward had suggested and followed the directions he'd been given. Not until he was in the elevator did he realize the hospital's antiseptic smell hadn't overpowered him. That, he decided, was a good sign.

Edward was waiting when he arrived and personally escorted him into his office. Greg noted with some satisfaction that Edward was as tidy and organized as he was himself. The physician's desktop held a pen-and-pencil set, a clock and a computer monitor. On the credenza behind him was a small collection of framed photographs. He recognized Catherine in one, beside a tall gray-haired man, obviously her husband.

"Your wife?" Greg asked, looking past him to the gold-framed photograph of a younger woman.

Edward nodded.

"I've been married three times," Greg blurted out, then wanted to kick himself.

His son had the good grace to ignore that comment. "I suppose you've guessed why I asked you to stop by the hospital."

Greg liked the fact that Edward was forthright enough to get to the point immediately. "I have an idea."

"Good," he said, and seemed to relax. "That being the case, I'd like to introduce you to someone very special."

Greg hesitated. "Now?" To his mind, there were

several things they should discuss before he met anyone important in Edward's life, but he was willing to let his son chart their course.

"If you don't mind, that is?"

"All right." Greg was simply grateful for this unexpected opportunity. His miserable attempt to see Edward earlier in the week had failed and humiliated him. Thankfully, Edward hadn't seen fit to remind him of what had happened at their last meeting.

Edward led him to the elevators and together they rode silently up several floors. They stopped at what appeared to be a children's ward. Greg frowned. Without asking any questions, he followed Edward to a room at the end of the corridor.

"This is Tanner Westley," Edward whispered, nodding toward the sleeping youngster. From the tubes and other medical equipment linked to the emaciated body, Greg could tell the boy was gravely ill.

"Should I know him?" Greg asked, also in a whisper.

Edward shook his head. "Let's return to my office and I'll explain the procedure."

Procedure? Greg wasn't sure he understood, but he accompanied Edward back to his office.

When they entered the room and resumed their seats, Edward said, "I can't tell you how delighted I was that you proved to be a match for Tanner."

"Match?"

"Bone marrow match," he said, eyeing Greg closely. "I assumed you understood the reason for my call."

"No. No way." Before he knew it, Greg was on his feet, emphatically shaking his head. "You want me to be a bone marrow donor? This is a joke, right? You saw for yourself what happens any time I have blood taken."

"But you did come into the hospital for the test. Surely you realized—"

"There's no way in hell you're going to get me to agree to this!"

"Please, sit down." Edward motioned calmly to the chair.

He made an effort to fight back his disappointment. This meeting had nothing to do with Edward wanting to know his birth father—it was all about what he could do to help some *stranger.* Greg continued to shake his head. No amount of talk, even from his son, would convince him to let someone stick another needle in his arm. Or anyplace else, for that matter.

"Before you refuse, let me explain the procedure."

"You have a snowball's chance in hell of talking me into this," Greg felt obliged to tell him. He sat down, crossing his arms defensively.

"Two weeks from now, Tanner will be placed in an aseptic room where all his bone marrow cells, both the good ones and the bad ones, will be destroyed by high doses of chemicals and radiation. This is the only way we have of completely eradicating the malignant cells."

"Doc, listen—"

"Let me finish, please, and if you still feel the same way after that, then . . . well, then we can talk."

Greg groaned silently and saw that he had no choice but to listen. Once Edward was finished, he would make some excuse and leave by the fastest route possible.

"This will be a dangerous time for Tanner, when he's most susceptible to infection.

"On the day of the transplant, the bone marrow will be extracted from you and stored in a blood bag, then intravenously transfused into Tanner over the course of several hours." He paused and studied Greg, who sat quietly, without moving. "Do you want to ask me about the pain or how the marrow is extracted?"

"Not particularly." He didn't need to know, didn't care to know, seeing that it wasn't going to happen.

"Most people are curious about the pain, and rightly so. I won't deny that there is some discomfort involved in this process, but I like to tell my donors that it never hurts to save a life."

Apparently Edward hadn't heard him correctly the first time. Greg wasn't doing this. *Couldn't* do this.

"I want to schedule the procedure as quickly as possible. As you can see, Tanner's health is failing."

Greg stared at him, wondering why Edward refused to understand. "Don't schedule anything for me. You'll just have to find another donor."

Now it was Edward's turn to wear a shocked disbelieving look. "You really won't do it?"

"Not on your life."

"It isn't *my* life or *your* life you're sacrificing. It's

that young boy's. He'll die without a bone marrow transplant."

"You'll find another donor." Greg stood, desperate to escape.

"No, we won't." Edward stood, too. "Do you think just anyone can supply the bone marrow for Tanner? If that was the case, I'd give him my own—but it's not. There has to be a match. You're that match."

"Don't see how I can be," Greg said stubbornly. He wasn't any relation to the boy.

"Why did you sign the release and agree to have your blood tested if you weren't willing to be a donor?" Edward raised his voice.

Greg dared not tell him the truth, dared not announce the real reason he'd come to the hospital.

"Did you take a good look at Tanner?" Edward asked. "He's only ten. He could be your son or even mine, and he's only got a very small chance of living without your bone marrow."

"And *with* my marrow?" Greg couldn't believe he'd even asked.

"There's a much greater likelihood that he'll see another Christmas."

Greg slumped back in the chair and covered his eyes with the heels of his hands. He didn't know what to do.

"Is he going to do it?" Mercy cried, pacing the area directly behind Edward's desk. "I can't stand not knowing."

"Shush! I can't hear." Goodness waved a quieting arm at Mercy.

"Shirley, do *you* know?" Mercy asked.

Shirley shook her head.

"He's going to refuse?" Mercy collapsed against a bookcase. "Has the man no heart?"

"Would you kindly stop that noise?" Goodness warned a second time. "I can't hear a thing."

"They're arguing," Shirley said. "And poor Greg has no way of knowing—"

"That Tanner is Matthias's grandson?"

"No, not just that," Shirley said sadly. The irony here had God's fingerprints all over it.

"No?" Goodness paused to look in Shirley's direction, clearly puzzled.

"What Greg doesn't know," Shirley told her two friends, "is that the boy is more than Matthias's grandson. He's Greg's chance for redemption."

Nine

Phil and Sandy Bennett arrived five minutes late for choir practice. Weaving his way between choir members, Phil climbed into his position on the riser, frazzled and irritated with his wife. Sandy might not have intended to make him feel guilty about Greg—but somehow he did. Well, not guilty exactly. A little uncomfortable, perhaps.

It wasn't until he opened the sheet music and started singing along with the others that he heard her. The blonde who sang first soprano was back! Gradually the tension between his shoulder blades relaxed. He knew it; she hadn't been imaginary at all. He waited until the last notes had died down, then casually leaned forward to speak to her.

"Where have you been?" he asked her, unable to disguise his excitement. Before she could answer, he asked another question. "What's your name?" It would have helped if he'd had a name to give Sandy. She knew a lot more of the choir members than he did.

"I've been busy," she told him.

"You're a member of the choir, though, aren't you?"

"I'm here."

Her hair was so blond it was almost white, and her singing voice . . . Phil had never known anyone who could sing quite like this woman. Her voice had a power and beauty that was almost unearthly.

"I've got to introduce you to my wife," he said while they shuffled through their sheet music, preparing for the next carol.

"What about your brother?" she asked. "Don't you want to introduce me to him, too?"

The music started before Phil had a chance to recover. "You know my brother?" he asked as soon as the last notes had died away.

"Oh, yes. I know a lot about you both."

"Who are you?" He didn't like the turn their conversation was taking.

"A friend."

Phil was beginning to wonder about that.

"You have Greg's loan application on your desk, don't you?"

How she knew that, he wouldn't ask. He'd been reading it that very afternoon just before he'd left the office, but only one person in the entire loans department was aware of it. He narrowed his gaze and studied this woman, who seemed to know more about him than she should.

"You haven't forgiven him for what he did to your mother, have you?"

"Damn straight I haven't."

"Then it might surprise you to learn that he hasn't forgiven himself, either."

"Pigs will fly before I believe he has one iota of remorse."

Frieda Barney turned around and glared at Phil. Someone else indicated her displeasure with his talking by pressing her finger to her lips. From the opposite end of the riser he could feel his wife's look burn right through him.

The music started again and Phil did his best to remain focused on it. The warmth he'd felt toward the beautiful willowy blonde had evaporated. By some corrupt means, his brother had finagled this . . . this spy into the church choir one week before Christmas. Greg always had been a good manipulator.

"You haven't spoken to him in all these years." A second voice came from beside him. This woman was slightly taller than the other. A second blonde? And one who sang? That didn't make sense. He closed his eyes, then opened them again, thinking he was losing his mind.

"Who are you?" he demanded in an angry whisper.

"The more appropriate question would be who are *you*."

"I know who I am."

"Do you?" the second woman asked. "Do you really?"

"You've always thought of yourself as the good brother," the first soprano chided.

"The churchgoer."

"The choir member."

"Yet all the while you've been plotting your brother's downfall, relishing it. You can hardly wait to see him suffer."

Female voices were coming at him from every direction. Not one voice, not even two, but three distinct voices. He thought he'd go mad if he heard another word. "Would you kindly *shut up*."

The room abruptly went silent. Everyone turned to stare at him. "I'm sorry," Phil mumbled. He could feel the heat rush into his face as he returned his attention to his music. He didn't know what had come over him.

Evelyn, the choir director, looked at him sternly. "Is everything all right?"

"Yes, I'm sorry. It won't happen again."

The director asked the altos to go over a particularly tricky piece of music while the others waited. They'd just sung the first line when the blondes started in on him again. "It's the season of brotherly love," the one beside him said. "I'm beginning to wonder if you know what that means."

Phil ignored her, refusing to let his gaze waver from Evelyn. At last the choir director motioned for the other sections to join in. These spies of Greg's could say and do what they wished, Phil thought, but he wasn't going to listen.

"You hide behind a cloak of decency all the while plotting your brother's downfall," the first blonde sang, the words fitting the music perfectly.

Phil's breath caught. He sincerely hoped no one else could hear these ridiculous lyrics.

"The good brother."

"The churchgoer."

"The choir member."

These three lines were sung as solos. The words seemed to linger in the air long after they'd been sung. Phil was convinced everyone knew the taunts were meant for him. Angry and embarrassed, he was about to get down off the riser and escape when he noticed the blonde beside him had vanished. He looked toward the row of first sopranos and saw that the other one was gone, as well. He'd never even seen where the third one had stood. How they'd left he didn't know. Didn't care. Good riddance. His relief was almost palpable.

Sandy began to berate him the minute they were in the car. "Your behavior tonight was appalling," she said angrily. "What's wrong with you?"

"Nothing." The car engine roared to life and he

drove out of the church parking lot, eager to put the entire episode behind him.

"Telling Evelyn to shut up was probably the rudest thing you've ever done."

"I wasn't talking to Evelyn."

"If not Evelyn, then who?"

Phil exhaled sharply. "The blonde."

Sandy was quiet for a long moment—unfortunately not long enough to suit Phil. "What blonde?"

"The one standing in front of me. Actually, there were two blondes. No, three, only I didn't see the third, only heard her."

Once more his wife grew quiet. "Phil, there wasn't any blonde standing in front of you," she finally said. "No blonde singing first soprano."

"Yes, there was." He didn't know how Sandy could be so blind. Did she honestly think he'd make up something like this? "Greg sent them."

"*Greg?* Your brother?"

"Who else would do anything so underhanded?"

Silence again. Sandy didn't seem to believe him, which irritated Phil even more. Of course Greg was behind this. He'd put those women up to mocking him in front of his wife and all these other people—and then disappearing. This was exactly the type of stunt his brother would pull, but Phil wasn't going to stand for it. Oh, no. If Greg was planning to make trouble for him, he'd be ready.

"What does Greg have to do with any of this?" Sandy asked.

"He's paid them to spy on me."

"Oh, Phil, that's crazy."

"They had to be spies to know the things they did. Only someone who's been watching me would know I have Greg's loan application on my desk. Furthermore these women seemed to know how much I'm looking forward to turning him down." He hadn't meant to say all of that, but it was too late now.

"You're rejecting Greg's loan application." The accusation in his wife's voice stung.

"He's a bad credit risk."

"Phil, this is your *brother.*"

"My selfish arrogant brother." Apparently his wife needed to be reminded of that. "Even at the end of her life, Mom was making excuses for him. Don't *you* start."

"You're jealous, aren't you? Both your parents are long dead, and you still think they loved your brother more than you."

"They did." It was a fact he'd lived with his entire life.

"Greg has come to you looking for help. It couldn't have been easy for him."

"It's not going to get any easier, either," Phil snapped.

"You sound . . . happy about it."

Phil entered the ramp leading to the freeway with a burst of speed, pushing the accelerator all the way to the floor.

Sandy waited until they were moving smoothly along with the traffic. "Greg's your brother," she said again. "And you have the power to help him."

Phil tightened his hands on the steering wheel. "You're beginning to sound just like those blondes, singing their solos, humiliating me in front of everyone."

"The blondes sang?" Sandy sounded worried.

"You mean to say you didn't *hear* them, either?"

"No," Sandy said. "Should I have?"

"Yes . . . no." Maybe it wasn't as bad as he'd first thought. "You're not just saying that, are you?"

"Saying what?"

"That you didn't hear them."

"I didn't," Sandy assured him. "But I still want to know what they said."

He sighed. "According to them, I like to think of myself as the good son and I wear a cloak of decency while plotting against my brother. Something like that." Phil checked the speedometer and realized he was speeding. As he slowed the car, he glanced at his wife, only to discover that she was staring intently at him. "Don't tell me my own wife agrees with them!"

Sandy didn't answer, but her silence said it all.

"Go ahead and be angry," he said, and noted he was speeding again. He seemed in an all-fired hurry to get home and he wasn't sure why. If anything, this argument was bound to escalate once they got there.

"I can only imagine how difficult it must have been for Greg to come to Pacific Union," Sandy said not for the first time. "Especially when he knew that you'd be the one who'd ultimately accept or reject his loan application."

Phil refused to dignify her comments with a response.

"Greg is coming to you for help."

Despite himself, Phil snorted with laughter.

"Oh, Phil, how could you?"

"Easy."

Right after Christmas he intended to call Greg into the bank. He'd leave him to wait and wonder during the holidays. When his brother arrived at the bank, Phil would have him escorted into his office. It would be the first time they'd been face-to-face since their mother's funeral.

Then he was going to personally deliver the news.

Ten

Christmas Eve Matthias stopped at the hospital following his grandson's bone marrow procedure. Gloria had spent the day with Tanner and called to tell Matthias that the transplant had gone well. Tanner was in an aseptic room Matthias couldn't enter. Only Tanner's mother was allowed to visit, and even then the boy was kept behind a protective plastic barrier. Despite that, Matthias couldn't think of anyplace in the world he'd rather celebrate Christmas.

Because of the unknown bone marrow donor, they actually had something to celebrate. The change in Gloria since the donor had been located was dramatic. The edge of fear was gone from her voice, and color had returned to her cheeks.

"Dad!" Gloria waved to attract his attention when he walked into the hospital lobby.

"Merry Christmas, sweetheart." He kissed her cheek.

"Dad, Tanner's donor is still here. Everything went as expected, but when he stood up to leave, he blacked out and fell against the hospital bed. He's got quite a gash on his head."

The donor had asked to remain anonymous and had given up today—Christmas Eve—for Tanner's sake. "I'm sorry to hear that. Is he okay?"

"He's fine. Said he felt foolish for causing all this fuss. He's in the emergency room, waiting for his wife to pick him up now."

"I'd like to thank him personally," Matthias said. "Do you think he'd mind?" This stranger, who'd responded to a newspaper article, had given his grandson a second chance at life. The only reward he'd received for his effort had been a cut on the head—and the grateful appreciation of Tanner's family. The least Matthias could do was sit with him until his wife got there.

"Well, I'll go and talk to him."

"If you don't mind, I'll go up to Tanner again."

"Good idea," Matthias said. He followed the sign that pointed to the emergency room; it led him to a large waiting area. Groups of people were scattered about. A lone man sat in a shadowy corner, his forehead bandaged. That had to be him.

He walked over. "Hello, I'm Matthias Jamison,

Tanner Westley's grandfather, and I—" Matthias didn't finish. He couldn't finish. All he could do was gape at the man he'd hated for fifteen years.

"Matthias, is that you?"

"Greg?"

In shock, they stared at each other for the better part of a minute.

"You're Tanner's grandfather?" Greg finally asked.

Matthias nodded.

Apparently Greg hadn't known of the connection between him and Tanner. The anger and hatred Matthias had lived with all these years flared back to life, racing through his blood like a shot of adrenaline. But to his surprise, it died a quick and sudden death.

Matthias claimed the chair across from Greg, astonished that he couldn't think of a single word to say.

"That explains it," Greg said, slowly shaking his head.

Matthias had no idea what he was talking about.

"Now I understand why I was a match for Tanner. It's because you and I are second cousins."

"You mean you really didn't know? That Tanner's my grandson?" Matthias had to ask.

Greg smiled wryly. "Not a clue. You're telling me that was Gloria I talked to a few minutes ago? Your Gloria . . . and Mary's?" As soon as he spoke, he seemed to regret bringing up Mary's name. "She's certainly changed from the little girl who used to race up and down the vineyard rows."

"It's been a long time."

Greg nodded. He splayed his fingers through his hair and winced when he touched the bandaged gash. His hair was almost completely gray now, but it looked good on him. "She isn't the only one who's changed."

"We've both changed," Matthias murmured, and leaned forward to rest his elbows on his knees.

"About Mary," Greg whispered. "I . . . I was wrong. I've thought of Mary, of you, so often . . ." He seemed unable to continue.

Emotion blocked Matthias's throat. It'd been so long since he'd cried that when the tears filled his eyes, they burned and stung like acid. Embarrassed, he blinked hard and looked away. "She died fifteen years ago and I still miss her. Doesn't seem right not having Mary."

"Can you forgive me?" Greg's voice was raw with pain.

"The Lord takes away, but He also gives. Mary's gone, but because of you, young Tanner's got a real chance at beating the same cancer that killed his grandmother."

"Mr. Bennett." Tanner's doctor joined them. Judging by the way he was dressed, he was about to leave. Not that Matthias begrudged him that, seeing as it was Christmas Eve. Edward, like everyone else, wanted to be with his family. "I just heard about your accident and I came to tell you how sorry I am."

Matthias, for one, was grateful for the distraction. It gave him a moment to compose himself.

"Not to worry," Greg said, as if the stitches in his head were of little significance. "It'll be healed in no time. Besides, I should've known better than to stand up without the nurse there."

"I did warn you not to be in too much of a hurry." The doctor smiled, then glanced at Matthias. "I see you two have met."

"We're old friends."

"Cousins, actually," Greg added, and because they needed an excuse to laugh they both did.

"I see . . ." the doctor said. "You have a ride coming for you?" he asked Greg next.

"Yes. My wife will be here any minute."

"If there's anything else I can do for you, don't hesitate to let me know."

"I won't," Greg promised.

Dr. Thorpe nodded. "I probably won't be seeing you again, Mr. Bennett, but I want you to know that I think you did a brave thing. A selfless thing. Thank you." With that he held out his hand. Greg stood and clasped it firmly.

"Thank you," he returned.

Greg slumped back into his chair, eyes on the retreating physician. "He's a fine young man, isn't he?"

Matthias heard a catch in his voice. "One of the best cancer specialists around." Gloria had repeatedly told him of the wonderful caring physician who'd been so good to Tanner and to her.

Greg's gaze lingered on Dr. Thorpe and his expression was oddly pained.

"You okay?" Matthias asked.

Greg's nod was slow in coming. "I will be."

Not understanding, Matthias frowned. "You want to tell me about it?"

"Perhaps someday," Greg mumbled.

The tension was broken by the sound of carolers. "Joy to the World" drifted toward them, the music festive and lively, a dramatic contrast to their current mood.

"Is it close to Christmas?" Greg asked, seemingly unaware.

"It's Christmas Eve," Matthias told him. Greg's eyes widened with surprise. "I didn't realize . . ."

The music made for a pleasant background as the two men continued to talk, mostly about Tanner and Gloria. Several minutes later Matthias brought up the subject of the vineyard. "I read about the fan leaf problems in your area."

"It wiped me out," Greg said.

That accounted for his cousin's haggardness and his beleaguered look, Matthias thought.

"A lifetime of work destroyed in a single season," Greg murmured.

"You're replanting of course."

Greg shook his head. "Takes capital, more capital than I can muster."

"Get a loan. That's what banks are for."

"You think I haven't tried?" Greg's voice rose. "I'm not a poor risk, at least not on paper, but money's tight. Tighter than I realized. Despite everything, I haven't been able to convince a single bank to give me a loan."

"I've been working with Columbia Wines up in Washington. The vines there are stronger, more resilient. Say the word and I can arrange for you to replant with those."

Greg shook his head again. "Hell, I'm sixty. Too damn old to start over now. Lately I've been thinking of selling out completely and hiring on with one of the other wineries."

That wasn't the answer, as Matthias was well aware. "You never could tolerate working for others. You like being your own boss too much. Besides, you're still young. I'm damn near seventy and I don't think of myself as old."

"Well, I can't get the financing."

"What about Phil? He works for a bank, doesn't he? He should be able to help you."

Greg shook his head. "He has as much reason to hate me as you do."

The carolers drew closer, drowning out any chance of further conversation. Matthias could only imagine what had caused such a rift between the two brothers.

Memory told him that Phil had always resented Greg's good looks, his social skills and sense of purpose. Whatever happened had been building for years. Matthias didn't doubt that Greg had played a role—but Phil had already been holding a grudge. Looking for a reason to justify his resentment.

Then, without warning, Greg rose slowly to his feet, almost as if he was being drawn upward against his will.

Matthias looked up and then he knew.

Phil saw his brother and Matthias at the same time as Greg saw him. His first reaction was shock, followed by unexpected compassion. Greg—head bandaged, features pale and drawn—stood beside Matthias Jamison, of all people.

Hardly conscious of what he was doing, Phil stopped singing. Sandy did, too. Slowly, involuntarily, he separated himself from the band of carolers. Almost before he realized his intent, he stood silently before his brother. They stared at each other, eye to eye.

Neither man spoke. For his part Phil couldn't find the words. This was what he'd wanted, what he'd dreamed about—seeing his brother, his sophisticated suave rich brother, broken and humbled. Greg was certainly humbled, but to his own amazement, Phil experienced no glee at the sight.

He was incapable of speaking. His mind had emptied, but his heart had grown suddenly full. His eyes filled with tears, and he struggled to hold everything inside.

Then, wordlessly, compulsively, the two brothers strained toward each other and hugged.

"What happened?" Phil asked when they broke apart. He was looking at his brother's bandage.

As if he'd forgotten, Greg touched his head. "Nothing much. It's nothing to worry about."

"Matthias," Phil said, glancing toward his cousin, "I didn't know you still lived in California."

"I don't. I came to see my family—and to thank Greg. He was the bone marrow donor for my grandson."

Greg had voluntarily given his bone marrow? Phil remembered his brother's aversion to needles—the way he'd always fainted in the doctor's office whenever he had to get a shot.

"I . . ." Clearly Greg was flustered. "I was a match for the boy. Matthias is our dad's cousin, remember?"

Phil nodded.

"How are you?" Matthias asked.

"Good," Phil told him, and the two exchanged hearty handshakes.

"You still work for Pacific Union, don't you?" Matthias asked him.

"Yes." Phil already knew what his cousin was about to ask.

"Can't you help Greg get the financing he needs to replant?"

"How are you going to answer him?" Sandy whispered, slipping her hand into the crook of his arm. Phil was sure the two men hadn't heard. He was reminded of other voices he'd heard that apparently no one else had. *You hide behind a cloak of decency . . . The good brother . . .*

"I'll see to it that you get your loan," Phil said,

looking directly at Greg. "Drop in after the holidays to sign the paperwork, and I'll arrange for the transfer of funds."

Greg just stared at him. "Phil," he began hesitantly, "you'd do that for me after . . ." Words failed him.

"It seems we both had a lot of growing up to do."

"Thank you," Greg said, his voice choked and low.

"Greg!" cried a female voice from across the room.

Phil turned and saw a stunningly beautiful woman at least twenty years his brother's junior come racing across the emergency-room waiting area. "Oh, darling, just look at you."

Greg smiled as the woman ran one hand down the side of his face and inspected the damage to his head. "How did this happen? Omigosh, you can't imagine what I thought when the nurse phoned."

Not answering, Greg placed his arm around the woman and turned to Matthias, Phil and Sandy. "This is Tess, my wife," he said matter-of-factly.

"Hello, Tess," Sandy said, and in that warm welcoming way of hers, extended an invitation to Christmas dinner. Matthias and Gloria were included, too; Gloria would be with Tanner for part of the day, but Matthias thought she could join them for a few hours.

"Can we, darling?" Tess opened her eyes wide. "You know how much I hate to cook. Besides, it's time I met your family, don't you think?"

Greg nodded, still smiling.

The women started talking, and soon it was impossible to get a word in, but Phil didn't mind. And from the looks of it, neither did Greg or Matthias.

"Isn't that the most incredible sight you've ever seen?" Goodness said from her perch atop the hospital light fixture. Shirley and Mercy sat with her, nudging each other as they jostled for space.

Seeing Greg with his brother, his cousin and his wife was heady stuff, indeed. Shirley couldn't have wished for more. Despite their antics, everything had worked out beautifully, and this hadn't been an easy case. Gabriel had made sure of that.

"I see you three are mighty pleased with yourselves," the archangel said as he appeared beside them.

"We did it," Mercy told him with more than a hint of pride.

"And all without involving the FBI or the National Guard," Goodness was pleased to report.

"There was that one minor incident with a hot-air balloon, though," Gabriel reminded her. "The Federal Aviation Administration is still looking into it."

Shirley noticed that her friends had suddenly gone quiet. "All in all, it's been a challenge." They'd brought the case to a successful conclusion, but Shirley was convinced it had taken more than a little heavenly intervention. "What's going to happen to Greg?" she asked, curious to learn what the future held for the man she'd once thought of as despicable.

In time she'd actually come to like him and wish him well. He wasn't as bad as he'd seemed at first glance, and she wondered if this was the real lesson Gabriel had been hoping to teach them.

"Well, as you can see he's mending fences with Tess," Gabriel said. Greg had his arm around his wife as they stood and talked to Matthias, Phil and Sandy.

"So their settlement meeting went well," Shirley murmured.

"Really well," Mercy said, grinning widely. "Okay, okay, so I joined them for a few minutes. Trust me, the meeting went better than either of them expected."

"They're getting back together," Gabriel continued, "and are determined to make a real effort to give their marriage another chance."

"Do they last?"

"With ups and downs over the next few years, but they always manage to work things out. They both decide that love, like most everything else in life, is a decision and they've decided to stay together."

"What about the winery?" Shirley asked.

"Greg does replant with the vines Matthias sells him, and in a few years Bennett Wines will once again be known as some of the area's best."

"Matthias and his grandson?"

"The boy makes a full recovery and Matthias takes frequent trips to California. When the grapes mature, Greg gives Matthias a percentage of the profits as a means of thanking him for his forgiveness and for his help through the early years. That small percentage is enough for Matthias to retire completely. And Gloria meets a good man, a new assistant winemaker hired by Greg. They eventually get married."

"I'm glad," Mercy said. "For all of them."

"What about Greg and Edward?" Goodness asked. "Does he ever find out that Greg's his biological father?"

Gabriel shook his head. "Edward doesn't change his mind about not wanting to know him, and Greg respects his decision. However, he is deeply grateful for the opportunity to have met the son he fathered."

Mercy smiled sadly as the carolers began singing "What Child Is This?" Shirley nodded in understanding.

"Now, are you three ready to return to heaven?" Gabriel asked.

Goodness and Mercy agreed, but with obvious reluctance.

"Can we come back next year?" Goodness asked as they drifted upward.

"We'll have to wait and see," Gabriel told her.

"Yes." Shirley linked hands with her two friends. "We'll just have to see who needs our help most," she whispered to Goodness and Mercy.

Center Point Publishing
600 Brooks Road • PO Box 1
Thorndike ME 04986-0001 USA

(207) 568-3717

US & Canada:
1 800 929-9108
www.centerpointlargeprint.com